Hers

30 Erotic Tales Written Just for Her

Hers

30 Erotic Tales Written Just for Her

by Thomas Roche & Alison Tyler

with a foreword by Mike Ostrowski
Correspondent, *Playboy Magazine*

Hers

Copyright 2003 by Pretty Things Press
All Rights Reserved
Cover Design: Eliza Castle

ISBN 0-7394-3100-5

Manufactured in the United States of America
Published by Pretty Things Press

Dedicated to Tracy—
TS

Dedicated to SAM—
AT

Mad girls must safely love as they may leave;
No man can print a kiss; lines may deceive.
                              —Fulke Greville, Lord Brooke

Contents

Foreword

I've never actually met Alison Tyler, but somehow I know she's a woman I could never say "no" to. When she recently asked me to write the foreword for her latest book, I was incredibly flattered—and of course, immediately obedient. Ms. Tyler and Thomas Roche have collaborated here on a collection of vivid, delicious and delightful short stories geared, on the surface, to the female perspective. However, most men will certainly enjoy them, too. Frankly, the audience for this body of work appears to be anyone with a healthy sexual appetite—which is, one hopes, nearly all of us.

To help satiate your appetite, please sample "Hers," a mouth-watering collection of erotica, full of believable yet often driven and somewhat naughty characters who sometimes find themselves in unusual situations. What's more, it is typically their passion that puts these people in those positions. As a result, the ordinary—plain, everyday objects, items, events and locales—consistently becomes extraordinary in these works. When you live your life with passion, the authors seem to suggest, nothing remains ordinary for very long. And that's an extremely heartening and inspiring thought that perhaps our founding forefathers would have applauded—life, liberty and the pursuit of passion.

There is tension of all kinds here, and humor, and desire, and longing—and a variety of other emotions and desires. In fact, there's something for everyone in this potpourri of sexy short stories, largely due to the unrestrained imagination and unbridled creativity of these two authors. Through it all, love, sex and mindblowing orgasms tend to prevail, as should be the case in good, lusty fiction. After all, every good story needs a climax.

I quite honestly found "Hers" great fun and very hard, if you'll pardon the pun, to put down. I suggest you peruse this collection alone—or perhaps better still, read it while cuddling in bed with someone you truly care about. And by all means, lay back, relax and truly enjoy the stimulating work of two masters of their craft.

—Mike Ostrowski
Correspondent, *Playboy Magazine*

Page Ten of the Employee Handbook

"We should stop," you say in that semi-sweet, semi-smug tone of yours. "Really, we should." I can tell from the taunting look in your lovely large eyes exactly how you want me to respond. I don't need any additional hints, but you continue as if I do. "It's against the rules," you add, gazing down at the floor as if shocked by your own naughty behavior.

"What is?" I ask, softly. "This?"

"Oh, yes," you tell me, playing coy now. "That's just wrong, wrong, wrong."

Now, I press you up against the wall of your office so that your palms are splayed flat on the wood-paneled wall. Then I slide that short black skirt up past your curvaceous hips. I take my time, because I like to admire the view. "Or this?" I whisper to you, my mouth against your neck, teeth poised and ready to bite. You can feel my hot breath on your skin and that makes you tremble.

"That," you insist. "That's just flat-out unacceptable."

"Ah," I sigh. "This is all getting clearer to me. You're saying that I'm just not supposed to do this—" As I speak, I gently slip your lilac satin panties aside. I love these panties. The black lace trim is a total turn on, and the way they perfectly and snugly fit your ass drives me wild. I know that you wore them for me, and that makes me even harder. The thought that you looked through all of the naughty knickers in your collection before choosing this particular set is an image that gives me pleasure.

Even though I do love occasionally absconding with your panties, slipping them into a jacket pocket to take home later and play with—this afternoon, I don't take them down, just push the smooth, slippery fabric out of my way, and my fingertips play out an immediate melody over your clit. For a moment, I make you lose your cool. My fingers stroke and tap, and you suck in your breath at the first wave of pleasure.

You can't be so clever now, can you? Not as the shining wetness coats my fingers, as I push back up and stand next to you, staring directly at you as I lick your juices off the tips.

"Oh, god," you groan. You can't suppress the shudder that throbs through you as you watch. Don't you love the way that looks? Me slowly tonguing away your sweet nectar.

"Is *this* wrong?" I ask, reaching my hand up under your skirt again to collect a fresh dose of your honeyed juices on the tips of my fingers. The first taste of you has made me hungry for more.

"No, don't stop—"

At your request, my fingers probe deeper, and I hold onto you with one hand, keeping you steady as I finger-fuck that sweet pussy of yours. I want you to be ripe and ready for me by the time I take my cock out. You need all the lubrication you can get, because I'm going to fuck you hard. Even harder than you're thinking about right now. I'm going to slam you up against the wall and make you forget how to be coy. How to tease me with those bedroom eyes of yours. Or should I call them 'boardroom eyes'?

"I don't know," I say, dropping onto my knees and bringing my face right up to your cunt. I breathe in, adoring the smell of your sex. The scent makes me dizzy with need. "If employees aren't supposed to date, then you probably shouldn't let me lick your pussy."

"Doesn't say a thing about that," you assure me in a rush.

"What do you mean?" I tease. "What are you implying? That we should side-step the rules? That wouldn't be fair to the rest of the work force, would it?"

"I'm just saying—" you start, but then you can't finish your thought because my tongue is already tripping along the seam of your body, playing you so sweetly. I know how to take care of you. I know the little tricks that you like best. My tongue makes several smooth rotations right around your clit, not actually touching that hot little gem, just brushing around it carefully. Slowly. And then, right when you think you're going to die if I don't touch you where you want, I slide my tongue along your clit in one long brush-stroke. You grip into my hair and hold on, shivering, so close already that I'm sure you can imagine exactly how good it's going to feel when I let you come. But I'm not letting you. Not yet. With a slow and steady pace, I resume those lazy, crazy, everlasting circles that make you want to sprawl out on the plushly carpeted floor and let me just lick you for hours.

"So," I say, speaking right up against your most tender skin. "What would page ten have to say about this—"

"No, nothing, nothing," you whisper, and it sounds as if you're begging. You're the one who brought it up, though. Remember that when I make you bite down on your lip to stifle your screams of pleasure. You're the one who opened the manual and used a bright lemon-yellow highlighter pen to illuminate all the different rules that we were breaking.

I can tell now that you're dangerously close, and so I stand and push against you. This is my favorite way to fuck, driving in from behind with both of us standing, but at first I simply let you feel my cock against you through my clothes. I want you to know precisely how excited I am. How ready I am for you. When you whimper again, I rip open my fly and pull out my rod. You're in the perfect position, back arched, poised to receive me. I wrap one hand around your mane of dark hair and tilt your head back so that I can watch your face as I slide inside you. That first deep push is unlike any other sensation. The way your body surrounds me is sublime.

God, are you lovely. Your eyes grow wider at the moment of penetration, and then get a faraway look, as if you've just arrived at some wonderful distant location. That exotic location called 'I've almost reached it.' We both know all about that place. And I'm going to take you even further—to a tropical island called 'coming together.'

Out in the hall, I can hear the bustle of secretaries working. Hear the voices and the sounds of their fingers on the keyboards. Their chit-chat on the telephones. I hear the low, gruff talk as different employees hurry past the room. Everyone's busy. Everyone needs something. Nobody will bother us, though. That's not even a tiny worry on my radar screen. Officially, we're holding a meeting, the two of us—an important, private meeting—so we can take our time.

Our time to do all the things I need to do to you. And I need to do so many things. Rutting forward. Driving hard. I need to make you crazy with the fact that you can't make noise. You can't be loud.

I want you to be warm and pliant, relaxed and ready, for what we're going to do next. Because this is what I think about it all, baby—if we're going to break those boundaries, we might as well do it right. Might as well really get down to business.

Don't you agree?

Under the Weather

Just after the soup, I realize you're not wearing much of anything under your cocktail dress. The top part, I knew about; you never wear a bra under this particular dress. It's one of the things that makes it so sexy, just a bit too low-cut to support even the slightest of bras, while being not quite thick enough to entirely hide the swell of your nipples under the thin fabric. It's decent, but just a little adventurous to wear to a dressy dinner party like this one. I know why you've worn it. I haven't been able to take my eyes off of your breasts the whole evening, of the way your nipples gently tent the fabric underneath. And that hasn't escaped your notice, which just makes them tent the fabric more.

The panties, I find out about when you reach to hold my hand under the table. At first I think it's just an affectionate gesture. Then you tug my hand into your lap. You snuggle forward on your chair, leaning back slightly so that your upper thighs are safely under the drapery of the tablecloth. Covering my hand with yours, you place it between your legs, against the satin stripe of your garters and the filmy lace-tops of your stockings. Then you inch it higher.

I resist at first, as my mind fights with the realization of what you're doing. Then, when you insist, I let you guide my hand up under your dress, where I feel in a rush of sensation the shaved softness of your pussy, slippery and open. You wrestle one finger apart from the rest and force it into you, laughing at a joke told far down the table—as if to cover your exhalation of breath as my finger penetrates you.

Then you pull my hand out from between your legs, your fingers entwined with mine, and casually bring it to your mouth to kiss it. As you might any other time, not caring that people are watching our casual exchange of affection.

Except this time, your tongue manages to trace a path up my middle finger and swirl around my fingertip, licking your juices. I'm quite sure that no one spots it, and if they did they probably wouldn't appreciate the lasciviousness of this gesture. But I notice it. You lean over and kiss me on the lips, quickly, your tongue tracing just the faintest path between my lips. I taste you, sharp and tangy and insistent.

When you let go of my hand and retrieve your own, it makes a quick detour into my lap, discovering that I'm as hard as you are wet.

"Excuse me," you say. "I'll be right back."

You disappear into the hall behind us, and one of our longtime friends, across the table, flashes an expression of concern.

"Is she all right?" he asks.

"I don't know," I say. "I better go find out."

Excusing myself, I turn quickly to hide my hard-on. When I hear the chorus of concerned sounds, I manage a shrug. "She hasn't been feeling well today—perhaps coming down with a little something. I'll make sure she's all right."

I make my way up the stairs, my cock throbbing in my pants as I near you. It's like I can smell you, the scent of your feral lust mixing with the tang of your pussy on my lips. I race up to the bathroom. The door is closed.

"Honey?" I call softly, for the benefit of those downstairs. I open the door and go inside.

You're seated on the bathroom counter, your dress a rumpled pool beside you, your thighs spread wide as you lean back against the big mirror. I'm on you in an instant, kissing you hard, our tongues entangling as my hand finds your pussy, finds it not just wet but gushing. I slip two fingers inside as you grasp my cock through my pants, tearing at my belt, getting it open. My cock's in your hands before I tear it from your grasp so I can go down on one knee and bury my face between your spread legs. I'm glad you turned on the fan to cover the uncontrolled sounds of your gasping as my tongue slides between your swollen lips, teasing your hard clitoris.

There's a knock on the door.

"Are you OK?" comes the voice.

"I'll be fine," you say, your voice husky. "I just need a minute."

We hear her footsteps going away, and I'm back at it, my tongue forcing its way into you, my thumb teasing your clit as you run your fingers fervently through my hair. I slide a finger inside you, then two, pressing hard on your G-spot as I lick my way up to your clit and suckle on it hungrily.

You've got my tie in your hand, pulling me up insistently as you slide off the counter and turn around, bending over at the waist. You drag me up against you, reaching behind to grasp my hard cock. I'm inside you even before I can get my fingers in your mouth, pressing them deep against your tongue as I close my mouth on the back of your neck, biting gently and breathing hard. I can feel your body spasm as you try to suppress moan after moan as I pump into you. I grab your carefully combed hair with my spit-slick fingers and hold your head tight as I bite your shoulder, gently pinching your nipples with my other hand. And then, as I sense you mounting closer, I reach down and work my fingers into the hollow above where my cock penetrates you, into the place where your clit throbs desperately with each thrust. It's time already, our illicit coupling having driven us both so high so fast that there's almost nothing we could do to keep from coming. You climax first, the muscles of your pussy clenching my cock in uncontrolled rhythmic pulses just an instant before I come inside you, shuddering with the release.

There's so little time for kisses, afterwards, but we share a few, as you lick my fingers clean. I splash cold water on my face and make sure I'm not too red from the exertion of fucking you. The toilet's flush covers a series of moans as we press our bodies together, hard, one last time before parting.

I zip up and buckle, leave you to get dressed, and rush downstairs just as they're bringing the main course.

"Is she all right?" asks the chorus of concerned voices.

She's more than all right, I want to tell them, but I manage to suppress it.

"She's fine," I say. "She'll be down in a minute. Just feeling a little under the weather."

More

What a fucking workout. I'd pumped iron until my legs were weak and my arms felt like jelly. Sometimes, when I've got a lot on my mind, I try to obliterate thoughts by exercising. Believe me, it works. I push myself until I no longer remember what problems were bothering me. All I know is that I can't go any farther, can't press any more. It's a good fucking feeling. After a workout like that, I feel pure. Today, I'd gone so hard that I was demolished.

Now, I was trying to reconstruct myself beneath the hot, hard spray of the shower. The water felt pebble-like against my skin. I stood, head down, breathing slowly, deeply, and as I rotated beneath the spray, my thoughts took a slippery trip to the woman who had put me through the hell I'd just endured.

You were new to the club, but obviously not new to training. With your panther-lean body, and a hunger for making your clients sweat through their preconceived boundaries, you had pushed me to my absolute limits. That would teach me to have sexist thoughts. When I'd caught sight of you, I'd been aroused, yes. What man wouldn't be turned on by your fantastic physique? But I hadn't thought you'd be able to handle me. Hadn't believed you could give me the kind of an intense workout a male trainer could.

But you came through. Oh, did you ever. Now, as the water rained over me, you were making me hot in a whole new manner. I couldn't help but wonder whether your gray eyes would remain that same deep unwavering iron as you put a lover through more erotic motions. My fantasies had their way with me and I slipped one hand between my legs and grabbed onto my cock. I had plans. I was going to jerk off quickly, give myself a little reward for a workout that hard. That's when I sensed a presence standing directly outside the smoked shower door.

Quickly, I shut off the water and looked out into the locker room. To my surprise, and extreme excitement, it was you...and you were naked, as well.

"Hey—" I started, but the words died on my lips. You grinned at me, and then climbed in the shower and turned the water back on. "What are you doing?" I tried next, even though I could easily see for myself. From the looks of things, my very personal trainer was now lathering me up with a bar of the luxurious oatmeal-scented soap provided by the gym. I stared in awe as you ran the soap over my broad chest, down my flat, muscled stomach, going on your knees on the porcelain floor of the shower and pressing the bar between my legs. Christ, that felt good. The hard bar of soap sliding firmly up and down my cock. I almost lost my balance, had to put my hands out on the wall to hold myself steady.

"Like that?" you asked.

Nodding, I closed my eyes as the hot spray from the shower rained down on the two of us, and as you now replaced the bar of soap with your knowledgeable fingers.

"Watch," you said next, "I like it when people watch," and I opened my eyes and looked down at you.

Your nails were short, not past the tips of your fingers, and they were painted a shiny, glossy turquoise blue, like the color of water in the deep end of the club's swimming pool. I stared down as you gripped onto my cock with one hand and cradled my balls with the other, and your nails gleamed like gems against my skin. You moved closer then, licking me, kissing me with your mouth open. Letting me feel your tongue, wet and sloppy against me. Easily, you swallowed me down as you moved your head back and forth, tickling me with your short, black hair.

"Oh, yeah," I moaned. I couldn't help myself. You were making me feel unreal.

With extreme finesse, you slid your tongue along my rod, and I forced myself to keep standing, my knees threatening to buckle. And fuck, you were good, expertly using your fingers, lips, tongue, to take me where I needed to go. With the water pounding down on me, the wetness of your mouth, I felt as if I'd arrived at some fantasy place where dreams could actually come true.

When the climax rocked through me, you didn't move, drinking me down like a pro. It took me several moments to get myself together after coming, and during this time, you sat back on your heels and looked up at me, a pleased expression on your face as if proud of a job well done. I stared at you through glazed eyes, but that didn't stop me from admiring your sweet form. Water dripped over your body, making you look as if you'd just gone for a nude run in the rain. You were both sweetly curved and slender, with small breasts that I could have cupped in my hands. You looked so fucking delectable that I wanted to go on my knees on the floor and wrap you in my arms. That might have happened anyway, since my legs were still threatening to give way.

You didn't leave me long to catch my balance, wanting more. Wanting your turn. You stepped out of the shower and motioned for me to follow. Quickly, we found the sofa in the dressing room, but before we continued, I raised my eyebrows at you. "What if—" I started. We were in the men's locker room after all. And even it if was a slow afternoon, someone was destined to interrupt us in the most embarrassing manner.

"I put the sign out," you said. "'Temporarily closed. Use the facilities upstairs.'" That problem dealt with, we fell onto the sofa in a sixty-nine, your mouth working again to try to seal itself to my body, my tongue lapping at your clit, my hands drawing your body closer to me. We took our time, sprawled out, wet from the shower, and hot from the languid way we touched each other. Now, I needed to pay attention to what I was doing, licking and lapping at your velvety mound of Venus, driving my tongue inside your pussy just to hear your moan.

You mimicked my style, playing with my cock in the same way that I took care of you. But then I upped the intensity by adding a new move. Sliding one finger inside your cunt, then two, I crossed my fingers quickly so that you would feel filled by them.

"More," you said, your request half a moan, half a sigh.

I immediately slid a third finger into you, then a fourth. God, you were hungry, swallowing me up, and I rocked my hand back and forth, stroking the inner walls of your cunt with my curled fingers, pressing in deep. You leaned your head back and said, "That is so fucking good. Don't stop. Please don't stop—"

Your body arched as the vibrations worked through you. I didn't let you down. I refused to stop touching you until the contractions had subsided, and you lay back on the sofa and stared up at the ceiling.

What next? I wondered. Where do we go from here?

And then you said the one word that started us all over again. The word you'd said after each rep in the weight room:

"More—"

In the Mood

When I'm in the mood, anything can set me off. And I mean quite literally *anything*. The sound of a faucet dripping will remind me of some soap-drenched, slippery shower escapade that we once shared—you naked and wet, smiling at me encouragingly as I spread shaving cream up your legs and prepared you for the razor. How steadily I moved, gently shaving your calves and thighs and then finally reaching the lips of your pussy—

Or the scent of tomato sauce cooking on the stove wafts over me, and that oregano-infused fragrance might remind me of the erotic adventure we shared in the deserted hallway of Tony's restaurant. What started with a simple kiss worked its way into a full-on grope, my hands under your dress, your mouth whispering urgent commands directly in my ear. We would have gone at it in the darkened corner of the hall, but we heard another customer headed in our direction and we had to move on to the parking lot, and fast.

This afternoon, it's not a sound, and it's not a smell, it's a visual enticement, or, in plain English, a magazine.

And it's all your fault.

You've casually left your fashion mag open to an ad for some slick-looking hair pomade, and the slogan catches me: *Sexy. Wet. Hot.* Of course, maybe it's a little more than only the cleverly crafted words on the page that captivate my attention. Maybe part of the advertisement's appeal is the blonde minx with the messy shag hair cut and the thick black eyeliner staring back at me. You look good in eyeliner like that. Rock 'n roll eyeliner, like Joan Jett or Shirley Manson.

Although I've got a million other things I should be doing, I can't make myself leave the room. I find an unstoppable urge to stand next to your rose-pink vanity, flipping quickly through the pages. A racy red push-up bra catches my eye for a millisecond—I picture you in the lacy lingerie, think of your lovely curves spilling over the top of the demi-cup. I like when you wear exceptionally feminine pieces, especially under unexpected outfits. Like overalls and a T-shirt when we wash the car. When go inside to change, I see that beneath the grungy attire, you've got on the sweetest little bits of nothing, just waiting for me to strip off you—

After a moment, I move on. Some ad for a girly soap product filled with strawberries and papayas gives me an image of you and me at the shore, you in your slutty little black two-piece waiting for me to rub you all over with oil. Wish I had a bottle of the oil right now, because I'd pour a river of it along the length of my cock and stand here, pumping away to the tropical island photograph—hammock, ocean, sun, and you in my head, my summertime chicklet.

Man, I'm hard, and all because you've left your ladies' magazine out where I can see it. How crazy is that? I'm mildly shocked when I realize that I'm treating your fashion magazine as if it were porn—but so be it.

I look at the clock and recognize that you're due home in less than a half-hour. I wonder what you'd think if you caught me getting a woody from this glossy serial. You'd tease me, no doubt, but you'd probably be into it. That's what I think when I pop my fly and start to stroke myself. That's what makes me feel more at ease, as I bring the magazine to the bed and sprawl out, one hand working piston-fast on my cock, the other tripping through the pages.

Now, I'm at a jeans ad. At least, I think it's a jeans ad. In the picture, a man is nuzzling against a sultry brunette, and she's wearing a bra and little else. So where are the jeans?

Ah, now I see. Where the picture ends, at the bottom of the page, you can just make out the start of her jeans in a blue denim pool on the floor. That's fine with me. I'd prefer to see the model without them on, anyway, so I guess that's the point—buy these jeans and your man will fuck you.

'Course, you don't need to buy anything for me to want to fuck you. Naked, dressed, in jeans or in lace, every time I see you, anyway I see you, I want more.

So where are you? If you were here, now, I'd tell you a story. I'd show you a picture in your magazine and describe the fantasy situation exactly as I see it. Your jeans off in a corner of the room and you, stripping slowly for me out of your shirt, your bra, and your panties. I'm not comparing you to the model, baby. You're far more attractive to me than she is. I'm just using the pictures as a starting point—a diving board from which to spring into a fresh set of images.

Oh, we're back on a beach now. So many of these ads use beaches. This is one for perfume, and the girl in the picture has long black curly hair, and she's rolling rambunctiously in the surf. I'd like to watch you do that. Get all wet and sandy while I take your picture. Let the waves lap at your skin, then let me dry you off and make you warm with my body on yours.

Now, what's this? An image for a liquor ad, the girl shimmying a silver bullet-shaped Martini shaker. She's got her little pink tongue out, licking her top lip, and her chin is dipped low in the sexiest pose. I love when you make martinis. You get your hips into the shimmy-shake action, and it makes me realize why Bond liked his drinks shaken, not stirred. There's something so sexy about that rotation. You don't mean to drive me mad, that's only a happy side-effect. And you know, you do make one kick-ass Martini.

Oh, look...here's another ad for alcohol. Those dirty-minded ad execs—what were they thinking? There are two girls and a guy in this ad, sitting together at a red leather booth. The scene is lit by candles, and the mood is one of intense seduction. But who's after who? This isn't your old-fashioned vodka ad, because here one girl is inching closer to the other. Is the company saying that if you drink their liquor, you'll have a threesome? Not a bad deal.

I picture me and you in the booth with the cuter of the two models. The redhead. Skip the drink, I'm thinking...let's have fun on the table.

Two more pages and here's a little coquette in a corset with a scarf wrapped around her hips. She's got her hair up in a loose bun, like someone from the 1890s, and a choker around her slender neck. She has all sorts of make-up on. More make-up than I generally like—but on her it works.

I picture you dolled up like that and decide I could get into the image. The glossy dark lips in do-me red. The hair coming free, gently, from your bun as I take you from behind. And on you, the outfit would work, too—I must think it would work, because I'm all kinds of close to coming now.

But that's understandable, isn't it? Because I'm in the mood.

And when I'm in the mood, anything can set me off—

String Bikini

Your bikini's really skimpy; I can understand that. After all, you don't want tan lines. But this is pushing it, even for you. It's barely a scrap of fabric on the bottom, a tiny little thong that plunges so low you'd be advertising everything if it wasn't for the good graces of your Brazilian wax. And in the back, it's nothing more than a string, sliding effortlessly between the rounded cheeks of your ass.

The top, though, is where it's really revealing. That's because you're busty—exceptionally so—and you've seen fit to wear a bikini that's a couple sizes too small. It stretches across your full breasts, revealing the firm buds of your nipples as they stand out, erect—making me wonder just what's running through your mind as you lay there, stretched out on your towel, your eyes hidden from view by mirrored sunglasses, your pale hair scattered across the grass of the back yard. It's a wonder the whole neighborhood doesn't think you're a shameless exhibitionist—then again, maybe they do.

And it's white, this scandalous bikini of yours. Meaning when it gets damp with your sweat, which it always does when you lay out on sizzling-hot days like today, it becomes even more see-through. I can see the swollen lips of your pussy underneath the skimpy fabric, and it does little to camouflage the outline of your breasts. Does it turn you on, showing off like this?

I know it does. It must, or why would you do it?

I'm sequestered in the living room, window wide open, high-powered binoculars trained on you. My eyes rove over the glistening slope of your flesh, the smoothness of your flat belly as you lay on your back, oiled up with suntan lotion and heated by the sun. My gaze caresses the smooth curve of your thighs, the full mounds of your breasts, the bikini leaving enough cleavage exposed that it almost shows your nipples. Your nipples, which seem to get harder as I watch you. Almost as hard as my cock.

You roll over, climb up onto your hands and knees. For a moment, your ass is pushed back toward me, the tiny crotch of the thong askew. I can see your bare pussy, exposed on the edge of the thong until you tug it back into place. It makes my cock throb, to see you plucking the thong out of your secret places, especially when you're bent forward like that, on your hands and knees as if you're inviting me in.

I reach into my shorts and wrap my hand around my cock. I start to stroke myself with one hand, the other holding my binoculars so I can enjoy the view as you stretch yourself out on the towel, face down, showing me your beautiful ass in all its flawless detail.

You reach up behind you, untie the straps of your top. It falls forward as you press your breasts to the towel, hiding your nipples, giving the barest illusion of propriety. Except that as you shift, I see your nipples, bare and naked, erect with arousal, tipping your full breasts. I stroke my cock faster.

I see you look over your shoulder, back toward the window where I sit with my binoculars. Perhaps, I would look away if there was time, but there's not. So I just sit there, stroking my cock as you look at me.

The look on your face excites me even more.

I watch your hand traveling down your side, as your hips rise ever so slightly and you spread your legs a little. I can't believe what I'm seeing. Your hand is inching its way under your body, finding the top of your thong—and descending into it.

With your hips raised like that, I've got a perfect view of your pussy as your fingers seek it, swelling the crotch of the thong as you stroke. I can see your fingers around the tiny slip of fabric, spreading your pussy lips to expose your waiting entrance. Two fingers disappear inside, and your body shivers as you fuck yourself.

Then your fingers slide out, and you're rubbing your clit. Now your hips are lifted all the way off the towel, in a perfect position for you to be fucked. You've lost all worry about the thong, now, and it's tucked to one side as you rub yourself eagerly. Every few seconds you let your fingers slip down to your pussy and slide two inside. You fuck yourself as you masturbate. Your ass sways in time with your thrusts.

Now your other hand has vanished underneath you, and your back arches as you cover one breast with your hand. You start to pinch your nipples, rubbing faster. You're not looking at me any more, but you know I'm watching. Your ass pumps in time with the thrusts into your pussy and clit, and you've lifted high enough that I can see one hard nipple, peaking your full tit, as you pinch the other one mercilessly. Your hips start working back and forth, fucking yourself onto your fingers. Your body glistens in the sunlight, and it's starting to gleam with sweat.

I pump my cock faster, watching you. More than anything I want to join you, tug that flimsy scrap of fabric aside and slide my cock into you, into your wet, waiting pussy the way you're begging me to. I know you'd moan for it, push yourself back onto my cock. I know you'd fuck back onto me until you came, until I came inside you.

Now, though, I stroke my cock, hovering on the edge as your body writhes in the sun. Now you've lost all sense of composure, and hauled yourself up onto your knees so you can roll over. You lay on your back, your breasts displayed plainly, naked, even more shamelessly exposed than the discarded bikini top left them. One hand is thrust deep into your thong, fucking your pussy, while the other hand works your clit.

When you come, your head goes back and forth so hard your sunglasses almost go flying. Your blonde hair scatters everywhere. As I watch you come, I feel my cock exploding, and semen spurts onto my hand, staining the front of my shorts. As you relax onto the towel, I know you've come hard—deliciously hard, the way you love to come.

You get on your knees again, adjust your sunglasses, and pick up the bikini top.

You stand and begin walking toward me.

I don't put away the binoculars. I just sit there in the window, my shorts wet with come, as you walk past me, your breasts bare, nipples still hard. You don't even glance toward me, looking ice-cold behind your sunglasses. You walk to the front door and come inside.

"What did I tell you?" I sigh as you come up to me, bend down and kiss me, your lips salty with sweat and bitter with suntan lotion. "You shouldn't wear that suit in the backyard—some pervert might be watching you."

You sit in my lap, the slickness of your oiled and sweaty thighs mingling with that of my come.

"I was counting on it," you say, and again kiss me tenderly.

Locked Out

In theory, the trip to Mammoth sounded like a good idea. Courtesy of my rich and generous best friend who has more than enough toys and likes to share, I was offered a highclass place to crash for the long weekend. "You'll get your screenplay done," Marlon promised me as he handed over the keys to his Mammoth Mountain retreat. "And then you'll ride down the diamond trails and work out your aggression."

"Ride?" I asked.

"Off-season, you can mountain bike down the ski trail."

"I don't even have a bike," I told him.

"All the stuff you need is there," he assured me. "You deserve a break, man. And, listen, I've thought of everything. Trust me—"

I sighed and stared at the key ring in my hand.

"Really," he continued. "You're never going to get your work done in the city. There are just way too many distractions for anyone to concentrate. You'll unwind as soon as you get out of town. Use the drive to focus your thoughts, get up to that mountain and chill out. You'll finish the script in no time."

So that's how it started. Me in my brick-red Jeep, cruising up the hills toward the elite retreat. And as soon as I got to Marlon's beautiful wood house, I thought that maybe he was right. Maybe the reason I'd been blocked for so long had been the noise of the city—and my roommates. The desire always to go for a run on the beach, or another cup of coffee, or a beer down at the Firehouse Bar on Main Street. Now, I would focus. I had only one more draft to get through, then

I could send this bitch of a script to my agent.

The first day, the words came quickly. Maybe it was the mountain air, but my thoughts had never felt so clear and precise. All Saturday, I spent at my laptop, taking short breaks to look out at the impressive mountains, then sitting back down again and settling into a rhythm of my fingers on the keyboard.

About four in the afternoon, I heard a car pull into the driveway next door. Semi-curious and needing and an excuse to stretch anyway, I walked to the window and peered through the sheer white curtain as you emerged. Man, did you look good in your gear. This was strange weather for summer. There was a harsh chill in the air, but the sky was blue and cloudless. Even with your body so well-bundled, I could see that you were tall and leggy, casually dressed in a pair of indigo jeans and a bright fuchsia parka with white trim. I watched you unloading your weekend supplies, and I waited to see if you'd look up at me. You didn't, oblivious to the fact that I was checking you out.

After a moment, I wandered back to the computer. I looked at the keyboard without seeing, my brain useless and thoughts on hold. Then I realized that I needed another peek. Back I went to the window. You were still unloading. I caught sight of your lovely face, your full lips, wished I could see your eyes but they were shaded by the silver mirrors of your aviator sunglasses.

It took every ounce of motivation to get me back to my desk. And now I focused fiercely to force myself to the finish line. But I found that I just couldn't think. I struggled to remember where I was in the story—had I just finished editing the page on the screen, or was I just starting? All I wanted to do was think about you. Your image was hot in my head. Were you an off-season vacationer like me? Or someone who lived here year-round?

Back I went to the window, peeking out to see what you were doing.

You were staring directly at me.

God, I felt like a Peeping Tom. It was obvious that I'd gone to the window to check you out, and now that you'd nailed me, I didn't know what to do. Sneak away behind the curtains? Wave? What would someone who didn't want to look like an idiot do in this sort of situation?

You answered the questions in my head by showering me with a huge beaming smile. Then you headed toward Marlon's front door, motioning with one hand that I should let you in. I hurried down the stairs to greet you. What could you possibly want? I couldn't wait to find out.

"You won't believe this," you said, brushing past me and into the hallway. You let your coat off with a sigh of relief, and I saw the tight black turtleneck beneath your winter parka, saw your dark hair spreading over your shoulders. Now, you headed back up the stairs, as if you owned the place.

"Lost my house key," you said, crashing into one of Marlon's overstuffed chairs. "And it's too late in the day to call the locksmith."

"Aren't they on call 24-hours?"

"Not off-season," you sighed. "I'm lucky they work weekends. I'll be locked out 'til tomorrow at 9."

I watched as you slid out of your boots and popped your feet up on the coffee table. "You mind?" you asked.

I didn't.

"Marlon's a friend," you continued. "I was so glad to see someone was over here. I would have had to go to the motel, and—being off-season—the only one available is a dive."

Here I am, a screenwriter, and yet I didn't have the dialogue to converse with someone like you. My tongue was tied. You seemed so at ease, making it clear that you were going to crash at Marlon's pad for the evening. When I continued to stare at you, you cocked your head and gave me another winning smile.

"Why don't you go get the bags," you said. "I can cook us dinner, at least, as a way to thank you for your hospitality."

Happy to have something useful to do, so I wouldn't just be standing there, staring, I went out and got the groceries. I brought them up the stairs to Marlon's huge kitchen, and as I unpacked the items I realized you'd bought dinner for two. Two steaks, two potatoes, a bottle of red wine, nice crusty bread. Were you expecting someone else? Didn't seem like it. I had questions, but I didn't say anything. You looked tired, and comfortable, so with your approval, I started cooking. We spoke through the open-hatch that led from kitchen to living room. As I grilled the steaks, you started a fire, then opened the wine. The scene was so cozy and enjoyable. So different from my fast-paced life at home. I couldn't remember ever being more at ease, especially with a stranger. A lovely stranger like you.

When I set the table, you came up behind me and wrapped your arms around me. And that was it for dinner. We made love in front of the fire, on the soft rug that seemed to have been set there for that purpose precisely. You looked so stunning, your long rich hair rippling around you as you gazed up at me. Naked, you were even more beautiful than you had been in your outer gear. In fact, I have to say, that you are one of those women who should just never wear clothes. The intensity of your figure managed to surprise me. You'd been so well-contained in the sleek black pants and slippery silk sweater. Now, you were all curves and lushness.

I wondered how we'd gotten here so fast, to this close-together point where anything you wanted, you said to me. There was no question about why I was into it. Christ, you're amazing. So sexy. So hungry.

I felt that on-vacation vibe from you. That feeling of doing something illicit with a stranger, because you'd never do it back at home. And it was a good feeling, I must admit. No holds barred. I took you in my arms and brought you down on my cock, so that we were sitting together, your legs overlapping mine, your arms around my neck.

"I like it like this," you said softly. "I like to stare into your eyes while I feel your cock inside me."

When you said 'cock,' mine throbbed within your body, as if it thought you were speaking directly to it. You took your time when you talked. You made the most of every word.

"You fill me up," you continued. "So hard. So deep."

The scent of your body was amazing. Rich and soft. I breathed in fiercely, my face against your neck, as I drove in even deeper. The fire crackled behind us, and the light from the flames flickered over our skin. I couldn't have gotten hotter than that. The power that flowed from you to me. The way you kept your eyes open the whole time. You were in the moment, and that excited me to the limits.

I had my hands in motion because I couldn't decide where to spend my time. I wanted to touch your breasts, to flick my thumbs over your hard nipples. Then I wanted to press my fingers against your clit, so that you could gain the contact you needed. So that I could take you where you wanted to go.

When you came, I saw each stage of the bliss flow through you. From the way your lips pulled back, your breathing changing, your body taking me in tighter. I held you through it, and then I turned you, so that you were on your hands and knees, facing away from me, and I fucked you like that. Just fucked you.

The release took me away. Coming and then leaning against your warm, naked body, caressing your skin with my skin. I was a million miles from anything I'd ever known. You brought me back gently. The way you rolled over afterwards and just smiled at me. Every moment with you was easy and simple. Nothing tense. Nothing structured.

We never did get to eat dinner. We just slept together on the rug, and in the morning, you called for a locksmith, and then when the phone rang, you headed outside to wait.

"So you enjoying your R&R?" Marlon asked.

"Met your neighbor," I told him.

"Met?" he repeated, and I could tell from the tone of his voice that he knew something that he wasn't saying.

"Well," I said, "maybe you know."

"Say that she lost her house key?" he asked with a laugh.

"Why? How'd you guess?"

"That's her favorite line," he said, "at least when she's in the mood. She told me that she'd be up this weekend. I thought maybe you two would hit it off. You looked like you needed some invigorating."

And that's when I realized that Marlon really *had* thought of everything.

Hot Stuff

We shouldn't be in here; I tell you that. It's 2:00 in the morning, well after the 10:00 closing time. But that doesn't dissuade you; you just put your face close to mine, caress my cheek, and say "Shhhhh."

One of the things you liked best about this apartment building was the sauna; you were willing to pay extra for it, even more so than the small pool and hot tub. The sauna helps you relax after a long day at work. And you're determined to enjoy it, I can tell, even though I don't think you have relaxing in mind.

Not that I'm arguing, really—just stating the obvious so I feel a little less naughty. But looking at you as you fit your key into the metal gate, I feel plenty naughty. You've slipped into your brand-new black bikini, skimpy in back and not much at all in front. It's the first time you've worn it; I helped you pick it out at the department store, surreptitiously slipping into the dressing room so you didn't have to parade around in next-to-nothing. I heartily approved of it when we picked it out together—and I like it even more, now.

You've got a brightly-colored Hawaiian-print beach towel wrapped around your lower half, and it's hanging off your hips like some kind of invitation. Just a gentle tweak of the half-tied knot and it would go sliding down your legs, leaving you naked except for the tiny patches of black. I can't take my eyes off the swell of your hips where the towel tries unsuccessfully to shroud them, the slope in the small of your back where your tattoo darkens your pale skin, or the way the bright towel falls around your calves. Your dark hair dances incitingly around your bare shoulders. I reach out and kiss your neck as you edge the metal gate open, going slow to minimize the telltale creak of the tormented hinges. The creak echoes faintly through the empty poolside.

"You're beautiful," I whisper, my lips on your neck.

"Shhhh," you tell me. "The people on the fourth floor can see us. Wait until we're inside."

Never the athletic type, I don't own a swimsuit. I'm wearing a long pair of boxer shorts that could pass for a swimsuit if one didn't look too closely. But I can already feel the head of my cock teasing open the fly, and I shift uncomfortably as I feel it hardening still more. The towel goes sliding off your hips as you squeeze through the gate, falling languidly on the floor. You bend over to pick it up and I'm enraptured by the way your ass looks, curving around that faint hint of black material. You hold the gate for me and I walk into the smell of chlorine. You close the gate very slowly, its latching just a quiet click bouncing off the apartment walls.

"I turned it on earlier," you whisper. "It should be good and hot."

You lead me over to the wooden door of the sauna. Gently, you tug it open. Hot air pours out over both of us. You click the light on and step inside.

"Won't they be able to see the light?" I hiss.

"Maybe," you say, beckoning me in to the sauna. "But I want you to see everything."

We close the door behind us and I feel the heat caressing me. You put the towel on the lowest bench and I sit on it. Before I know it, you're sitting in my lap.

"Feel the burn," you sigh, and laugh softly. "I know I'm feeling it."

You lean back hard against me, turning your head so you can kiss me. Our lips meet and I taste your tongue, wriggling into my mouth. I feel my cock hardening all the way, now, against your barely-clad ass. You rub back and forth against my cock. When our lips part and I bend forward to kiss your neck, I can already taste the salt of your sweat.

I reach for your breasts.

"No," you say, playfully swatting my hand. "Just sit for a minute. I want you good and hot."

It's torture, sitting there with you in my lap, your ass pressing against my hard-on and the scent of your body intoxicating me, mingling with the smell of redwood as I breathe in rhythmically.

"You set it really hot," I whisper, already stifled and uncomfortable.

"Shhh," you say. "Just feel it."

And I do, as beads of sweat start to stand out all over my body. My boxers are already soaked, with sweat and with the tiny bead of pre-cum your wriggling butt is coaxing out of my hard cock. Worse, your body heaves as you take deep breaths of the scalding air, and I can feel the lush curves of your shoulders and back rubbing against my chest. Your skin glistens in the light, and I want very badly to run my hands all over it—but I hold myself back, waiting for your cue.

"God, I'm fucking turned on," you moan softly, and slip out of my lap. You turn to face me and my eyes devour your sweat-shimmering body. I love the way the moist bikini top clings to your breasts, your nipples standing shamelessly for me to admire, telling me just how turned on you really are. Slowly, you tug the cups down over your breasts, teasing your nipples as you ease your tits free. You lean forward over me, putting your knee up on the redwood bench and bringing one nipple to my parted lips.

"Don't touch," you whisper when you sense my hands coming up behind you to cup your ass. "Just suck."

I take your nipple into my mouth, droplets of sweat

running onto my tongue. I gently suckle as you moan, your shoulders thrust back and your body arched so no part of you touches me except your nipple. I taste your sweat like it's my only nourishment, my hands flat against the beach towel as I fight the urge to stroke your foot. Your nipple grows harder in my mouth and your moans come gradually louder as my tongue flickers your hard bud.

"Reach behind me," you say. "And undo my top."

I do as I'm told, gently pulling the catch. Your top is strapless, so the second the stretchy, soaked fabric is freed it falls inert into my lap. You sweep it away with a quick stroke of your hand.

I keep suckling on your nipple, now fully aware of the swell of your breasts against my face as you gently slide them back and forth, teasing the other nipple into my mouth. Your breasts are smooth, but not slippery; the soaked top absorbed your sweat. It takes a moment before the rivulets of sweat start running down from your face, neck and shoulders.

Suddenly, the dam of your desire seems to break and you slide forward, your upper body touching mine. From the first touch it feels unrecognizable, so slippery that the familiar friction is almost non-existent. Your body moves against mine with no resistance, like some sort of physics experiment staged by a particularly kinky grad student. I moan softly at the tickle of your breasts on my chest as you slide down until you can stroke your face against my belly, licking sweat from my flesh.

The shorts, now soaked, come open easily, my cock popping through the fly. You take it in your mouth, licking from top to bottom, the moisture evaporating strangely from the flesh of my shaft as you work my shorts down over my ass. I lift my body just enough for you to pull them down, my cock slipping back through the fly as you push my shorts to my ankles. Then you're back on my cock, mouth clamped hungrily around the shaft as you slide your breasts wetly against my thighs. When you hear my moans mounting faster, your mouth comes off my cock and, before I know what's happening, you're standing slumped against me again, both of us sweating fast enough that even the friction of our touch hasn't wiped away the sweat.

"Take my bottoms down," you tell me. "Don't touch."

I gingerly peel your soaked bikini bottoms off your ass; they fall effortlessly to your ankles and you kick them away. Then you're on top of me, your knees planted firmly on the beach towel, your legs spread as you press your slippery body to mine and lift your pussy to find the head of my cock.

If anything, your pussy is slicker than the rest of your body. My cock goes in easily, bringing a moan from your lips. Your body slides against mine, your sweat drizzling on me like a hot shower. Your hips move up and down as you push yourself onto my cock, bending forward to press your lips to mine. As we kiss, sweat dribbles over our lips and I taste our sweat mingling, salty and sharp. Your moans grow louder as you fuck me, and you come so fast I almost wouldn't know it was happening if you didn't whisper "I'm coming....I'm coming....I'm coming!" as you pound onto me. I lift my hips to meet yours, each thrust hitting hard as I feel the contractions of your pussy, tight around my cock. Then I pull you hard against me, lost in the sensations of your slick breasts against my skin as I come, too, releasing myself into you, my moans matching yours in intensity. You grind slowly to a halt, leaning heavily on me.

Which is when I notice the scent of smoke mixing with that of your body and of the redwood. I look over to the cache of hot rocks, and your bikini bottoms resting atop them, languid spirals of smoke rising in the hot air.

"Oh, no," you sigh, pulling yourself off of my cock. You walk over and gingerly pluck your swimsuit off the rocks.

"Oh," you say, dropping the ruined garment. It's now a half-burned, half-melted twist of synthetic fabric. You sit in my lap, naked, and look sadly at your new swimsuit.

"Well," you say. "I guess it's back to the mall. Do they even *make* fireproof bikinis?"

"I don't think so," I say.

You turn and kiss me.

"Well, then. How do you feel about skinny dipping?"

The Shoes

It's the shoes. No doubt about it. No questions asked. Those slinky, sexy, fuck-me red patent leather shoes with the ankle buckle have managed to completely demolish me. I'm not exaggerating. I'm harder than a table leg, and all because you've gone out shopping, indulging in your passion for fantastic footwear while fueling my dirty little fetish.

Who would ever have thought a pair of shoes could have so much power over a strong, willful man like me? Well, that's easy to answer. *You* would. Because you know—you know all about what I like, don't you? You know that I can take just so much teasing, before I lose my cool.

But I don't cave easily. Not for just anything. Little frilly dresses do nothing for me. Expensive lingerie is wasted money in my opinion. I like to tear through outer wear and inner finery. But talk to me about shoes. Shoes are different. Shoes are magical.

These shoes flat-out rock my world.

First, there's the buckle that goes around your ankle, fastening those dangerous creations in place. The buckle itself is a work of art. It is almost as thick as a dog collar, and made of heavy leather that I imagine stroking with my fingertips. I think about doing this while you're wearing the shoes, catching your skin on either side of the buckle and sending a shiver through you.

I don't know what you think about when I'm down there on the floor in my foot-worship motif. Are you just as excited as I am by this crazy fetish of mine? You must be, because you indulge me. Oh, do you indulge me. The shoes you buy.

Those naughty, indiscreet shoes...and under the shoes, your sweet, pretty feet. But we're not there yet. Oh, no. We're not to the feet by a long shot. We're still at the shoes.

Now, let me discuss the heels on these shoes—my god. Spikey heels so that the shoe bends into a little arch, and—Jesus, I'm losing it here. It's the most amazing thing. The way a simple pair of shoes manages to transform your entire being. These are so high that I know they will make you stand differently. Make you walk like a queen, in that haughty way of yours. Or like a stripper, I guess, how confident you are in your body when you're wearing shoes like these and nothing else. You are a wonder to behold.

So, now you understand. I've come clean. I've confessed. Although, I'm sure you figured it out. The way I hang close to you when you're putting the final touches on your outfits, hoping that you'll pluck one of my favorite babies from the rack. Because the special shoes are all I want. Well, you, of course. You in those shoes. Nothing but the shoes. Standing there in the doorway and waiting for me to be able to move toward you. Heart pounding. Blood pumping.

Sweet thing, I can't control myself when you're in a pair of your lovely, high-heeled shoes. I just want to sweep you up in my arms and spread you out and start from toe upward, and then return from head downward. That's how it should be. How it has to be, especially with these new red shoes. You'll keep them on the whole time. I know you will. You have to. Keep them on for me. I'll make everything else worth your while if you keep the shoes on.

I'm not one of those guys who pays attention to the trends. I don't know if these are this year's or last year's style. But I do know that when I first saw them in the box this afternoon, nestled there in the white tissue paper, I knew you had to wear them tonight.

It was lust at first sight.

What was I doing in your closet? Looking up there in your shoe boxes? You know—you have to know. Why else would you have taken Polaroids of the shoes and taped them to the outside of each box if not to tempt me? For me those pictures are better than your average porn. I see the shoes, each individual pair, and I want to open box after box and press my face into the leather, smelling both the scent of the shoes and the scent of you. When I first found these ones today, I felt like a little kid who was sneaking around searching for Christmas presents in July. That's not what I was doing—truly. I wasn't on one of my shoe rampages, where I spread all your pairs out in a circle and stroke them one by one. No, I was innocent for once, simply reaching for something in the back, my old black belt because my new one broke, and I glanced up and saw them.

Tell me they weren't there yesterday. I'd have noticed. I'm sure I would.

I saw the picture and I reached for the box and brought it down. And bam—instant hard-on. Instant arousal. I ran my fingers over that shiny smooth surface and I thought of your pampered feet sliding into the deep curve of the inside, and I had to sit down on the bed to steady myself. But I was still holding onto the shoe and the box, and then I rustled through the white crinkly tissue paper and found the other Polaroids you'd taken. Not just displaying the shoes this time, but showing off your feet in the shoes. Teasing me, weren't you? And that's when I called and left the message.

"The shoes. The red ones. Tonight."

So now, here I am, waiting for you, knowing somehow that you won't let me down. Knowing, even more importantly, that you must have bought these babies as much for me as you did for you. Because you know me. You know what I'll do for you when you have shoes like these on your pretty feet. I will make you come like you can't imagine.

When my tongue and fingers are finished with their initial interest in the shoes, I will bestow the same amount of aroused intensity on your clit. And I know, from the past, that you'll be so dripping wet when I make my way to the split of your body that you'll tremble and shake in my embrace.

Your shoe fetish matches my own, doesn't it? You like what I give as much as I like to give it.

Worship. Adoration. Your feet command it; these shoes deserve it.

I'm pacing now. Can you believe it? Waiting and hoping. Imagining exactly what it's going to be like. I can hardly control myself. Why is it taking you so long?

When you call out that you're ready, well, it's almost more than I can handle. I open the door, hands trembling, and see you stretched out on the bed, Polaroid at your side, legs crossed, and nothing—fuck me—nothing on you at all except those beautiful red shoes. And I make some sort of whimpering noise that sounds nothing like my normal voice, and I go on my knees on the carpet and get my face up close to heaven. That's what it is. Heaven.

I lick from the base upward, saving myself, telling myself to go slow. I trick my tongue along the instep, and I push it in under the curve of your arch, and you squirm and squeal. It tickles, huh? But sweetly, right? Perfect.

The scent of the leather is making it hard for me to stay calm. I am lost in the heady aroma of new shoes. Sometimes, when we're at a department store together, and you pull me after you into the ladies' footwear department, I have a difficult time hiding my hard-on. All those shoes. All lined up. And those adorable little mirrors on the floor, as if the shoes want to look at themselves. Christ, if I owned a store like that, people would be having sex on the floor all the time. Constant shoe orgy. Can you imagine?

Yes, I know you can. Because you're lifting your hips now, grinding against the mattress as I lick my way along the delicate curve of your ankle, skimming the leather band as I work. And then I treat you, since you have treated me so well, to a quick little suckle at the place you most need it. I move quickly to your split and lick your clit in rapid hungry strokes—and what have we here? Isn't your clit all engorged and ready? You're so excited, sweetheart. You've been growing wetter by the second, haven't you? Just getting ready for me. Getting ready for what I want to do to you. I give over to your needs for several minutes, licking and lapping, even nipping at your clit before making my way back down again, now actually coming to a point where I need to undo one of the shoes. Take it off you. Take it off quick and press my face into the shoe to smell it better. Then I see how much you love me—you've had a pedicure and your toenails gleam in lovely candy apple red.

Oh, god. Oh, baby.

I press my cock against your instep as I drag in a breath of the shoe. I am on fire. I am out of control. I am going to come quickly, I realize, and then I'll slow down and we'll take it from the top. I've been so hungry all afternoon, since I first saw these lovely shoes. So ready. So desperate. So if you don't mind, I'll just jack off against your foot, with this shoe in hand, and take care of my needs and then I'll take care of yours.

The shoes. Man, those unbelievable shoes. So wonderful. Who would have thought? So unique in their color and design, and that buckle— oh, that buckle. I am almost there. But I need more. I have one shoe against my cock now, and I move to press my face to the split of your body once again, licking the crest of your clit while still smelling the scent of your shoe. And then you say the words that manage to take me over the top.

"Tomorrow," you purr, "there's a shoe sale. Stilettoes, you know? We'll go together. Would you like that, baby?"

I can't even answer. You know me too well.

Away from Prying Eyes

I watch you all through dinner. You and your friends are a giggly group tonight. Someone is celebrating something important. I can't tell precisely what. A promotion? Engagement? A trip abroad? The four of you are drinking frilly pastel concoctions and driving the men in here wild with lust. How? That's simple. You don't seem to have eyes for any of us. You're all so busy, intent on each other. And that's damn sexy. At least, in my book.

Of the foursome, you're my favorite by far. You have a special look. Dark eyes, long dark hair, pale skin. Plus, you aren't all dolled up like your buddies. You have party clothes on, yeah, but not skintight. Not too glitzy. You're refined, and I like that. Especially, because I think your elegant outside appearance protects an inner rebel. Why? How could I guess that without knowing you?

Simple. You catch my eye throughout the evening. Not boldly. Not often. Just occasionally, when I bring a second round of drinks, or ask if I can delight you all with a free dessert. The others are outrageously flirtatious, but you have a calm, easy smile, and you win my attention. I don't want to shoot the round for your buddies, but I do, in order to give you a free drink. I don't care if they like the whipped cream and chocolate fudge cake, but I want you to try it.

When you make your way down the hall and then up the stairs to the pay phone, I make my way after you. I don't know why. There's no reason to think you want me to follow. But when I reach the top of the stairs, I see you waiting. Not talking on the phone. We're by ourselves, and you reach for me, wrap your arms around my neck and bring me down for a kiss.

I'm hard from your lips on mine. I'm rock-solid hard. The kind of demanding hardness that you can obviously feel against you, because you let loose with a low, sexy chuckle and then rub your hand over the bulge in my slacks.

Do that again, I want to tell you. *Go down on your knees and do that with your mouth. Just do that.*

There isn't much time for us. I know that. Patrons at other tables will be looking for me, and for their food, and your friends will start to miss you eventually. Doesn't matter that they're far from sober; they'll realize at some point that your chair is empty. But we have long enough to kiss. To kiss in an urgent, hungry way that's like no kiss I've felt before—your warm, wet lips on mine. Your body so sweetly pressed into mine. I lift you up, cradling your hips in my hands, and I let you feel how much I want to be inside you.

So much.

You give that laugh again as you slide your body up and back against me. We're still clothed, and yet I feel as if I know just what it would be like to fuck you. How good it would be. I know the way your hair will look, mussed around your face, the way your cheeks will flush. When I set you down for a moment, I push my fingers up under your skirt, graze your pussy lips under your panties, and then bring my hand back again to my lips. You watch me lick your juices off my fingertips, and this makes you sigh and your eyes glow darker. What I'd give to go down on my knees and push your panties aside. To eat your sweet pussy while you stand, leaning against the wall, holding onto my shoulders to keep yourself steady.

What types of soft moans will you make when you come? Will you cry out? Call out nonsense words? Or will you get low and soft, cooing out your pleasure? I am almost to the

point of fucking you, just forgetting everything else and
fucking you—

Then there are footsteps on the stairs, and I block you
from view with my body and adjust myself as you take your
faux position by the phone, dropping in coins and lifting the
receiver. Dazed, I hurry back to my job, and playing catch-
up keeps me busy for long enough to regain my sense of
self. My erection lessens, and I manage to make it to your
table with the bill without tripping over myself.

The rest of your girlfriends seem completely unaware.
You take the bill and say, "On me, tonight," and why do I
think that you're talking just to me? The women you're with
put up just a mock fight. They don't mind letting you pay—
you all must have the kind of friendship where things like
that even out over time. You have plans of your own; I can
tell that from looking at the expression on your face. What
you don't know, is that I have plans myself. Because there's
a surprise waiting for you—I've comped your group's entire
bill.

I see you open your mouth, about to say something to
your buddies, but then you shake your head as if you've
decided on a different course of action. You reach for your
wallet, and then make your way over to the bar. "Getting
change," you call out to the ladies. I see you over there, but I
don't approach. Your party gathers up their belongings, slides
into jackets, shakes out long hair. You make an obvious effort
not to look at me this whole time. I wait until the busboy
clears the table, and then I walk slowly back to where you
were seated.

There's a surprise for me, as well. I open the vinyl
envelope that holds the slip of paper saying, "No charge."
On the bottom you've written "thank you," and then your
name, and your phone number, and those words again in
your even handwriting— "on *me*, tonight."

And I think about what it will be like when I get off work, and how you'll feel when I slide inside of you—away from prying eyes.

That New Car Smell

You're the one who encouraged me to buy it; perhaps I should have wondered. Except that I'd longed for a new car, that uniquely American desperation for the new car smell. But you're the one who comments on it when we slide into the bucket seats.

"I love that smell," you say. "How do they get it to smell like that?"

"Some sort of perfume they manufacture in Detroit, maybe?"

"This one's German, though."

"There goes that theory."

I want to burn rubber pulling out of the dealership, but I manage to remain respectable. When we hit the highway, though, I can't resist flooring it.

"Easy, cowboy," you smile at me. "Those horses belong to you."

I look over at you, excited by the way your white sundress drapes around your slim frame. I can see your bra strap and the faintest hint of lace around your neckline, and it makes me want to take that dress off you, make love to you in the afternoon light of our apartment. I always want to do that on Sundays, but this Sunday is special. I've promised you a drive in my brand-new car.

Out on the freeway, I take us up to eighty, passing SUVs, sports cars and ancient, puttering sedans alike. You coo at the way the car hums along smoothly, not even the suggestion of a wobble or a bump as I take the exit to the mountain highway.

"You've been watching too many sports car ads," you smile, your eyes bright as you enjoy the scenery. "Remember that old advertiser's adage."

"What's that? 'There's a sucker born every minute'?"

"Closed course: do not attempt."

This is my favorite road to take on my motorcycle, its curves tight but even, the sprawling view of the wooded valley one of the most beautiful things I've ever seen. I take the curves quickly, and I see you clutching the edges of your seat, staring straight ahead.

"Sorry," I say, easing up on the gas. "I'll slow down."

"Please don't," you tell me.

I smile and lean on it a little more.

We've got the windows down, and the scent of pine wafts in—but that doesn't diminish the new car smell, its telltale scent mingling strangely with the perfume of nature. The curves are easy, the purr of the new car inviting me to experience life to the fullest and all that.

That's when I feel your hand in my lap.

"I have a secret to tell you about me."

"You don't say."

Your hand tenderly kneads my crotch. I feel myself hardening in my jeans. We hit a straightaway and I glance over at you; I can see your nipples gently tenting the fabric of your white sundress.

"That new car smell? It makes me wet."

By now I'm fully hard, my cock pulsing with the strokes of your fingers.

"You don't believe me."

"Sure I do," I tell you.

You sigh sadly. "I don't think you do."

Your hand comes away from my cock and goes to your side. By then, we're back in the curves, so I can only steal surreptitious glances at you as you pull up the hem of your white sundress and slide your fingertips under the sides of your panties. You pull them down and off. Casually, you toss them out the window.

Your dress is still pulled up, almost to your waist. I watch, fascinated, using my peripheral vision. You spread your legs slightly and move your hand between them, blocking my view of your pussy as you stroke it. You slip first one finger, then two, inside you. When you ease them out, you lean against me and bring your hand to my lips.

"See? I'm telling the truth."

Your fingertips draw a path around my lips, moist, then slip into my mouth. I taste your pussy, sharp and rich and erotic. I take a deep breath as I negotiate the curves flawlessly, the taste of your cunt inspiring me to greater speeds.

"You still don't believe me," you sigh.

"I believe you, I believe you."

"No, you don't," you say, and take hold of my wrist. "Aren't you glad you bought an automatic?" you ask me as you press my hand between your legs, working my fingers into you. Now I know for sure you're telling the truth—not that I had any doubts. You're so wet I can feel the slight dribble of juice leaking out onto my hand. You pull my fingers out of you and guide my hand to my face, pushing my fingers into my own mouth so I can taste you more.

"Keep your eyes on the road," you tell me, and unbuckle your seat belt.

I want to tell you to stop, want to lecture you on highway safety and the inherent risks of getting a blow job at sixty miles an hour on a mountain road. But even if I could speak with your head in my lap, I couldn't utter a word as I negotiate each curve with both hands gripping the wheel, my attention focused with great difficulty.

You get my belt unbuckled and my jeans open. I'm hard already, much harder than I expect. Your lips close around the head of my cock and your head begins to bob up and down as your tongue swirls around the head.

"You better not make me come," I say hoarsely.

"Don't worry," you say, your breath passing warmly over my moistened cock. "There's only one place you're going to come." Then you're back on my cock, your mouth eager and hungry as the curves rock you gently back and forth. Your tongue feels hot on my skin, and I can feel the head gently teasing the back of your throat as your fingers wrap around the base of the shaft, firmly stroking. I have to hold my eyes open wide to keep from shutting them and moaning in pleasure—which would be a very, very bad idea, under the circumstances.

"Roll up the windows," you tell me as your lips hover on the end of my cock. "I want to smell it."

That's one of the many great things about this model: Electric windows, driver-side controls. the windows go humming up smoothly, and you take a deep breath. "Mmm," you sigh. "Cock and new car smell. Who would have thought they'd go so well together?"

Then you're swallowing me, all the way, desperate for my hardness in your mouth. Your dress is still pulled up, and when I glance down in the straightaway, I see the inviting curve of your ass with the thin white fabric tucked alongside it.

That's all I can take. I pull into the turnout, and the new car rolls to a halt.

You look up from my lap, your lips glistening. "But honey," you ask me. "Don't you want to try out your new car?"

"Definitely," I say, and pop the lever of the reclining bucket seat.

If you were just an inch taller, it would be impossible. But when I reach out and grab your waist, I'm not thinking about that. I'm thinking how good you'll feel on top of me, how hard I am for you. I guide you, your legs spread around my waist, one knee wedged uncomfortably into the space between the seat and the emergency brake, which I've forgot to set. I pull it, giving you the extra inch of clearance you need to settle down on top of me.

You're even wetter than when I felt you; the head of my cock slips so smoothly between your pussy lips I almost can't feel it at all. But when it teases open your entrance and you slide down on top of me, pushing my cock into your cunt, I can feel it, all right. I can feel it so acutely I throw back my head and moan.

"Don't you love that new car smell?" you ask me, your head tucked into the crook of my neck, your hair dancing around my face, its perfume all roses and feminine sweat.

"All I can smell is you," I sigh, breathing deeply.

You push down onto me, my cock striving deeper as your hips begin to move in time with mine. I'm not telling the truth, really—in the heat of the sealed car, I can smell everything: you, me, the car. My hips rise off the bucket seat as you reach down to touch your clit.

"Oh," you gasp. "Oh, God—"

You're more turned on than I've seen you in weeks. As your finger works small circles around your clit, you reach up with your other hand and pull the straps of the sundress off your shoulders, taking your bra with them. You pull both down to your waist and slip your hand out, then back down to your clit. You press your breasts into my face, and I kiss them hungrily, suckling your nipple into my mouth as I feel the pressure of your hand on your clit.

"Yes," you tell me. "Just like that—"

Then you come, hard, the contractions of your pussy beckoning me deeper inside you. Hovering just above me and deftly proving the strength of your thigh muscles, you whisper "Fuck me," and I do, my hips pumping wildly as I seek my own climax. When I reach it, you moan even louder than you did when you were the one coming, your hips matching my thrusts until my whole body tenses, then relaxes, and you snuggle down onto me again, my cock softening deep inside you.

You kiss my neck, your tongue trailing against my skin. You take a deep, deep breath of new car smell.

"A few more times like this," you sigh, "and it won't smell like new car at all."

"I can live with that," I say.

You look down at me, a smile brightening your sweat-moistened face, your eyes dancing with excitement.

"So can I," you tell me.

Damsel in Distress

"These panties?" I ask, dragging my fingers over the soft emerald green velvet cut into a butterfly shape. "You like these?"

You nod, lost and confused by all of the different decadent choices. I understand your sense of awe, because by anyone's standards there are a huge array of possibilities here. Even a knowledgeable lingerie connoisseur would be dumbstruck. After all, I've taken you to the most dreamy undergarment store in California. It's an exclusive environment with a required membership fee and a ID card flashed before admittance. Every option available is tacked to the red satin wall. Leather and lace. Bright colors and sequins. Feathers. Rope. Vinyl. Silk. If you've ever fantasized about lingerie before, you'll undoubtedly find your mental creation here. Someone else has had the same dream, the same concept of how to dress a girl, and they've created it and put the piece up for sale.

"Do strippers shop here?" you ask me, indicating two stunningly well-endowed girls working their way along the far wall.

"*Everyone* shops here," I tell you, pointing to an intricate bustier I want to buy for you.

"No, really?" you're blushing at the thought. Here you are, a plain cotton panties type of girl. And that's fine. I love the way you dress. I love the fact that your whole underwear drawer is an homage to simplicity. Clean lines and carefully chosen colors.

But I have a vision, and I need to make it come true.

"This one—" I point out.

The salesladies are dressed to display the wares. The one who's helping us has on a pair of red vinyl thigh-high boots, a glistening set of shiny tap pants, and a black leather vest worn over nothing but her ripe, round bare breasts. You sigh as you follow me toward the wing of dressing rooms, and then you give me a half-frightened look as the saleslady shakes her head at me. I'm not allowed back here with you. I have to wait on the plush sofa—wait and think about what you're going to be sliding into. This rule was made for obvious reasons. Everyone would be fucking in these dressing rooms if given the opportunity. The place screams sex. Who wouldn't want to steal away and do it amidst a pile of racy lingerie?

It takes a minute for the girl to lace you into the creation. From where I'm seated, I can hear the conversation going on within your dressing room. It's obvious that the redheaded saleschick is helping you every tie of the way. She tells you to suck in your breath, and I do at the same time, fantasizing about how the corset will look on you. I can see it as clearly as if I were in the dressing room with you: your breasts lifted, so plump and firm above the top of the tightly fitted creation that they almost look like someone else's breasts. Some model in a magazine. In a moment, you are transformed, and I know that you're going to like the change, but I don't realize how much until I see the look on your face.

"Oh, yes," you say, nodding. "We'll take that—"

I smile, pleased that you're as into it as I am. But when you grin at me and move to go back and slide into your street clothes, I shake my head. I have other plans. "No, we'll take that now," I say, "leave it on."

And you give me a curious look, but the saleslady understands perfectly. "You're not going to make it home," she whispers happily in your ear before continuing on her way to ring us up at the register. "Don't worry, honey. It won't be the first time that someone's used our back alley—"

You grab your purse and blouse and stand next to me while I pay. Then you try to slip your shirt on, but I take it from your hand. "No," I say again. "You're going out with me like that. You look like a—"

"Stripper," you murmur, but the salesgirl says, "Princess," correcting you.

"That's right," I agree. "A princess. A fairy tale princess."

"And you're—" you start

"Her prince," the saleslady interrupts, before you can say anything. In my mind, I can hear your voice filling in the blank, "extremely horny," or "overly hard," but you don't have to say it out loud. You can see it in my eyes, and when you lower your gaze, in my slacks. I pull you by the wrist out the back door to the large parking lot, and I know that you're thinking that the saleslady was right, I'm going to fuck you right here, but I don't.

"You do look like a princess," I say as I help you into the car. When I get into the driver's side, I finish the statement. "Or a damsel," I continue, "one who will soon be in distress."

I see your cheeks light up with an instant pure-cherry blush, and I let you think about what that means while I drive us home. When we get to our apartment, I lead you quickly to the bedroom, and I have you cuffed on the mattress without a word. Then I take my time and slow down. All the way home I wanted to fuck you. And, truthfully, every moment we were in the store, I wanted to fuck you. But now that I have you right where I want you, I need to take my time. Carefully, I pull the ponytail holder from your hair and spread your long tresses down past your shoulders. I take off your mules and work your jeans down your thighs, so that you're wearing only the corset and a pair of your standard white panties.

Oh, do you look amazing. I knew somehow that this type of outfit would work for you—the dreamy, old-fashioned appeal of the black corset against your milky pale skin. The way your long loose hair ripples in such soft curls over your shoulders. And the look in your eyes, that longing look as you wait to see exactly what sort of distress I'm planning on putting you through.

The sweetest kind. No worries, my darling, the sweetest distress ever.

Still silent, I reach for you and slide you over my lap. You know what's coming. A second before I slip your panties down, you moan. Don't you like to be my bad girl? That's an easy question to answer: yes, yes, yes. But now, with you in this bit of finery, this unusual costume, I feel as if we're part of a play. You're the princess who must endure the humiliation of a spanking before her prince can care for her. You're truly the damsel in distress as my hand meets your naked ass and leaves a stinging mark there. And then another. You have the type of skin that colors easily. I adore heating your rear for you, listening to the sweet moans that you make each time my palm connects.

Usually, I'd spank you fiercely, for much longer than I am going to this afternoon. Usually, I'm not so completely sexed-up, and I can take my time. But after only ten smacks, I just about lose it. There is something intense about playing this game while you're in the corset. I don't know why, but there is.

I spread you out again, your wrists still over your head, and I fuck you. Climb on top and fuck you. And from the initial thrust, I learn that you're as ready as I am. The whole shopping trip was decadent foreplay, and now, as I slide in your juicy wetness, I see that I've excited you to the point where you are crazy with need. The choosing clothes, the dressing up, the spanking—all of it.

My cock slips back and forth, and you arch your body up to meet me. Then I place one hand between us, searching out your clit, and as I fuck you I pinch that little pearl gently between my fingers. That makes you groan and toss your hair so that curls cover your face. Then you buck and your eyes are clear again and staring into mine. You come one beat before I do, and I ride the wave of your orgasm to my own finish line.

As I take the cuffs off and rub your wrists, you grin up at me. "I saw this other thing at the store," you say, blushing already.

"You did?"

"This Merry widow," you say. "The saleslady thought it would look really nice on me—" and I realize we'll be making a trip back to the lingerie store soon, and that you may amass a collection of colors among your standard blacks and tans and whites.

Most Likely to...

Under the bleachers, the whole view of the world changes. The sunlight ladders, creating interesting shadows, dark moving stripes along fair naked skin. Under the bleachers, the grass smells moist and wet. The fragrance of nature is just one beat away from the smell of sex.

Under the bleachers, is where I found you at our ten-year college reunion. When I slid beneath the white-washed boards, you were already waiting. We had a standing appointment, didn't we? Meet you at this time, on this date...and there you were. You didn't let me down. You were as ready as I was.

It didn't take you a second to come into my arms. Your lips were warm and soft on my own. Slowly, I kissed you, working my mouth down the hollow of your neck, breathing your scent as I slid my lips even lower. I could feel your smile, but I didn't know exactly why you were grinning. My fingers found out your secret after only a moment: beneath your sophisticated black cashmere trenchcoat, you were wearing your cheerleader outfit.

"Still fits?" I asked, looking up at you as you stood and unbuttoned the rest of the coat and then spread it out on the grass. I reached for you and I spread you out on top of your ankle-length coat. "Still fits perfectly," I repeated, answering my own question, as I looked you over. Vermillion sweater with our team emblem emblazoned on the chest and that short red-and-white striped skirt.

Although you looked so hot in that outfit, I have to admit that I couldn't wait to undress you. In moments, your sweater was over your head and tossed aside, so that you were down to the white cotton bra beneath. I left the skirt on you, flipping the pleats in front and bending down to press my mouth against your panty-clad pussy.

"So sweet," I murmured as I licked you through that clothing barrier. "God, you're so sweet." Then I stopped talking, focusing on the issue of making you come under the bleachers. That was the only goal in my mind. We didn't care that the rest of the reunion clan might be missing us. We had far more important things to do.

"I've been dying to do this for you for years," I told you, pushing your little skirt completely aside and burying my face between your thighs.

"More. Tell me more."

"I remember how you tasted, and I wanted to tongue you, to lick up and down your pussy lips and ring your clit with your lips."

"Now—" you urged, begging with your body. "Do it now. Please—"

Instantly, I was on you, sliding your body into the perfect position. We were like kids, so anxious, so ready. We spent our afternoon on the emerald green blanket of grass, with me finally sliding your panties aside so that I could press my bare face against your naked pussy.

You groaned and arched upward when you felt my tongue meet your nude skin. The power flooded through you. The power of pleasure. I don't know how you didn't scream. I remember all about you screaming—

Whenever one of our dormmates was out, you and I would invade the room, working quickly to strip out of our clothes, making the most of whatever precious few minutes we had to share. We were creative, weren't we? And then once, in the showers after a game. Christ, you had nerve didn't you? Yeah, I remember.

In fact, I remember a lot about everything. You leaving school to go off to see the world. Exactly how you put it. Peace corps. And then working for the UN. And all sorts of adventures that you kept me posted of in emails and letters from far away places. "Wasn't it crazy?" everyone said. There you were, the perfect college girl. I mean, perfect. President of your Sorority. Cheerleader, for god's sake. Nobody thought you had a brain in your head, did they? But you showed them all, and you did what you said.

And me? I followed the game plan, going back to my home town and joining the family business and missing you. But not realizing it right away. That's the truth. I liked hearing about you, and I spent my time with my buddies and the occasional girlfriend, and then finally, after one personal email, I realized that I was always on hold waiting for you.

And I remembered our pact—meet here. Ten years. Rain or shine.

Now, in the late afternoon light, you had me move so that you could echo what I was doing between your legs. I was quick to pull out my cock, and then get into position so that it bucked toward you with its perfect rounded bulbous head, begging with a simple gesture to be sucked. You took pity on me, fulfilling my fantasies immediately. The wet feeling of your mouth meeting my hardness was like an explosion within me. Nothing has ever felt that good. Nothing since the last time we found ourselves in the same position. Slip-sliding against one another. Girl, you really know what you're doing. You always did.

The heat and softness of your mouth on my rod was like a wet dream come true. I worked not to get overly charged up. I tried to think dull thoughts so I wouldn't end things too quickly—not yet. I wanted to make this afternoon last and last and last.

So I thought about old times. Don't things change?

Back in school, our frat house did that whole high school-ish game of trying to figure out what would happen to everyone when we left college safety for the real world. I was voted most likely to succeed. But succeed at what? I never had any true idea. You had your sights set. When you decided what you wanted, you went after it. Now, ten years later, you'd got what you wanted. Away. But you were back. Just for tonight? Or for more than that?

My rock of an erection strained toward you as we moved so that we were once again face to face. I kissed you deeply, my hands tracing along the lines of your face, cradling your chin, and then I was telling you secrets. Those secrets that you share in the moment of heated passion.

"I missed you," I confessed. "Really missed you."

You didn't answer. You simply leaned forward and brought me back down on you, my strong chest, powerful body. I pushed your glossy dark hair out of your eyes, leaned up on one arm and stared down at you.

"Did you think about me?"

"Yes. Oh, god, yes—"

"Tell me what you thought—"

"This," you whispered, "I went through total withdrawal."

I liked the way you said it, with your classic grin, because I had a fix for your problem. "Let me give you what you've been missing," I said, moving so that I was able to enter you, to slide into you. That sensation was immediate and overwhelming.

We were outside. No holds barred. Nobody to worry about. I let myself go, fucking you with abandon. Listening to you moan for me to do it harder, faster.

"They were wrong back in school—" I murmured, finding it difficult to talk, but doing my best. "I shouldn't have been voted most likely to succeed—"

"What do you mean?" you asked me.

"I should have been voted most likely to come—" and as I said it, I did just that, and you followed just a moment later, climaxing hard and long on my throbbing cock. I held you to my body, sealing you to me. Old times and new times, blurring together in bliss.

Sticky Sweet

Maybe the food thing has been done before. Done up and done down. Inside and out. But I have to make it clear that I just don't care. Sometimes the very best activities have been worked through previously, planned and shared among the masses. Is whipped cream cliched? Maybe so—but maybe not. Maybe every lover has the occasional craving to be a naughty chef in a kitchen without rules. Or to become one with a meal—a main course, a delicacy to be feasted upon.

That's how I'm feeling this evening. I've got this yearning, this hungry need to play with my hands and my mouth and your luscious body. I am desperate to turn you into an edible confection. Which isn't to say that you're not delicious all by yourself, because you are. Sticky and sweet. Rich and creamy. You are my favorite aphrodisiac by far. More than oysters. More than chocolate. And yet...every once in a while, I like to play with my food.

My desires aren't deeply hidden. I don't try to deny the passion that I have for playing in the kitchen. But I remain silent all evening. Although I know exactly what I want to do, I need you to discover my fantasy for yourself. It doesn't take you long. You don't have to be Miss Marple to know exactly what's on my mind as soon as you open the fridge. Among the abundance of healthy ingredients residing on the wire racks, the zucchinis and cucumbers, vine-ripened tomatoes and fresh basil, your eyes catch sight of the white and red can of ready-to-use whipped cream.

"Really?" you murmur, hand on the cool canister already. "This is what you want tonight?"

"Really," I nod, and now that you know, I can't stop myself. I push past you, surprising you, and I reach for the can, quickly shaking it to get it ready to foam.

"For dessert?" you ask. "With berries? On ice cream?"

You're teasing me. You have to be.

"You—" I explain. "I'm hungry for you—"

Your eyes widen as you smile, and I see that I was right. You are just one big tease, taunting me each step of the way because you know you have me in your power. If you'll let me recreate you, I'll take care of you in the most divine and decadent manner you can imagine.

"Here?" you murmur.

I nod. Right here. Right in the center of the kitchen. With the round globe over our heads and the smells of ripe foods all around us. There are no words as I strip you. Just your eyes focused tightly on me and my hands shaking as I pull your cobalt blue cotton dress over your head and then remove your simple, shiny bra and panties. I tell you to lie down, right there on the cool linoleum floor, and you do. No questions. No problems. I slide a folded-up dish towel under your head and I watch for a moment as you tremble at the chill of the floor. I've got the heat up high, and I know that you'll grow accustomed to the strange sensations in no time. Besides, I'm planning on getting your mind off the atmosphere.

You gaze at me as I reach for the bananas.

"You're not going to fuck me with that," you say, giggling.

No. I'm not. But I'm also not interested in making you into just another average sundae. Where's the creativity in that? No, I'm going to turn you into a perfectly created, intensely rich, dreamy confectionery banana split. You have to understand—banana splits are very sexual desserts. There are the bananas, of course, which have their unique, rather easy-to-fantasize-about shape. And then, there are the toppings: whipped cream, chocolate sprinkles, and maraschino cherries, my personal favorite.

With your eyes so intent on me, I go to work. I peel the ripest bananas and cut slices of them to place on your nipples and in a line along your belly toward the lips of your pussy. This is an edible road map of where I am going to go this evening. Then I reach for my whipped cream. Using the canister, I aim and squirt, making you shriek whenever the cool foam hits your skin. Oh, does that look sweet, almost like lace, or some frilly rickrack to hem a fancy dress. I make lines and designs, maybe going a little over the top with the cream, but unable to stop myself.

Next, I dust your entire body with chocolate sprinkles. These are almost like freckles, and I use them liberally. You are dripping and wet, trying to keep in one position in the center of the floor. You don't know if you should talk to me while I'm cooking. I can tell. Your eyes follow me as I warm some chocolate syrup, testing over and over until it's the perfect temperature to dribble onto your naked skin. You moan at the feel of it, sticky and sweet along your ribs, the base of your belly, that indent between your collarbones that I so love to kiss.

The next touch? Maraschino cherries, of course. But I need a little snack first. A little reward for all of my hard work. And I know that you need a treat, too. I bend to eat the bananas from the lips of your pussy, while you wriggle and beg me to make you come. You've been so good, baby. So quiet and patient, letting me play with you—and on you—letting me decorate you. I should take pity and bring you to the cusp, right?

Yes, right—but not yet.

Now, I place a few of the deep red cherries, stems out, in your lovely honey pot. You tense down and contract on them, so that when I tug the cherry stems, you groan at the sensation of tug-of-war within your pussy. I let you win this game. I leave the cherries inside of you and start at the top, ready to devour my most dreamy creation.

Hungry for you, I lap the whipped cream from your breasts, dine on the cut bananas coated with syrup and sprinkles, and move down again to your pussy. Now I pull the cherries out with my teeth and devour each one. You are so desperate for release by now, have been waiting during my entire creation, but I'm not finished. There's still the matter of chocolate sauce.

Remember, baby? What's a banana split without the hot fudge topping?

"Oh, god," you moan as I spread your legs wide apart and begin spooning the still-warm syrup over your cunt lips. The chocolate makes drizzling designs on your skin, turning you into a work of modern—and edible—art.

After each spoonful, I lap you clean, or close to clean, and then I spoon another gob of drippy syrup on you. The gooey chocolate makes its way between your pussylips, and you beg me to let you come. I can deny you nothing. Not with you all sticky and messy like that. You're ready for anything. My tongue, my fingers, my cock.

The floor is a soupy mess of ingredients, but we don't care. I lick and suck the chocolate from the split between your legs. You are nearly wild with pleasure, and I slide my fingers inside you while I suck on your clit.

"More," you whimper. "More, please...."

I suckle and drink chocolate syrup from you, flicking my tongue between your parted lips to catch every drop until finally, shuddering, your hips beating out a wild rhythm on the kitchen floor, you come, sticky and sweet like nothing I've ever tasted before.

Strangers on a Bus

It had been two years since my last serious love affair, six months since my last orgasm with a real flesh-and-blood partner instead of my horny fist, and I was getting desperate. Truly desperate. Usually, I can control my desire. I handle my sexuality they way I handle a thermostat: I turn it off or on when I want to. That ability comes with age and experience. If I need a quick release, I always have my hand to turn to. That and a squirt of expensive lube.

But now something had happened. During one morning bus commute, I'd caught sight of you, and once you entered my plane of vision I couldn't get you out of my head. The sensation was instantaneous, as if a photo negative had become imprinted in my mind, so that each time I closed my eyes, I saw you. For the first time in my life, no amount of masturbation could control the images of what I wanted to do with you. Or, more honestly, *to* you. I could see it easily in my X-rated fantasies, the two of us meeting somewhere— anywhere—and fucking. Just fucking. In my daydreams, you were equipped with the same untamed libido that I possess, and you would insist that I take you. Seriously take you. The first time, anyway. Quickly and fiercely, so we could get that initial screw out of the way before we slowed ourselves down, before we worked to make it last.

Even with these images dancing through my head, I couldn't manage to get myself off. I rubbed for what felt like hours with no relief of climax. I tried all of my tricks, using a silk scarf to caress my balls while I pumped with my hand. Squeezing lotion in my palm and then cradling my hard-on as I slid my fist up and down. But no—nothing. This was a completely new experience for me. I'd never been unable to deal. In all aspects of my life I am cool and contained.

You'd ruined me. Without being the slightest bit aware of that fact. You controlled my world.

I spread out all the facts mentally before deciding that I would find you again. I had to. But how? I'm not the kind of person to write in to one of those "missed connections" sections of the local Weekly.

You: *gorgeous, high-class girl on the bus.*

Me: *horny bastard desperate to meet you. To fuck you. To spread your creamy thighs and lick, and lick, and lick. I want to taste you. To dine on you. I want to press you up against a wall and drive my cock inside you. And when we're done, I want to do it all over again.*

Yeah, that would go over great. That wouldn't frighten you off at all. No, there had to be a better plan. So finally I came up with the only plausible solution I could think of: I would find you by following your route. I rode the bus until the driver seemed apprehensive of me. This isn't entirely unreasonable. I cut a fairly startling picture. I'm six feet tall, hard-bodied, and I wear my dark hair razor cut. After my fourth day-long journey on our local transportation system, you got on. You were wearing leather, as you had been before, and your long, blonde hair was done in two tight braids. I saw everything about you: the deep berry hue of your lipstick. The kohl pencil around your dark eyes. Saw the way your breasts looked in that simple T-shirt and open sweater, the way your ass looked in those leather pants.

I moved to the free seat at your side and stood next to you, looking down. "Are you taken?" I asked.

You glanced up at me, and for a moment I thought I saw a flicker of recognition there in your eyes. "Is this *seat* taken?" you repeated, correcting me. Then you waited, your lips parted slightly, for me to answer. I shook my head emphatically and then repeated my question.

"Are *you* taken?"

You could have done anything then to change the course of our destiny. You could have moved away, or told the bus driver I was annoying you, or pulled the cord that would have signalled that you wanted off. I wouldn't have followed you. Believe me when I say that I'd have chalked it up to fate, and moved on with my life. I would have gotten over you eventually, I'm sure. But until you answered, I still had a chance.

To my delight, you blushed a perfect pale-rose hue and lowered your eyes and I knew from that moment that you were mine. But still I needed to hear your answer. I waited until you said, "No," in a low, semi-aroused, semi-reserved voice. "No, I'm not taken."

I understood your trepidation. I was a stranger, after all. A complete and total stranger. And you must have been able to tell from the way that I was looking at you that I wanted something from you. Something aside from the chance to sit by your side. Desperately, urgently, I wanted something.

"Good," I said, sitting down in the empty seat.

I felt the heat of your body pressed against mine. You look damn good in those leather pants, and you know it. I can tell. The skin of them against my Levis was enough to make me want to shoot. That and the fact that I'd been dreaming of you since the first moment I'd seen you—day dreaming and night dreaming. But somehow I held myself in. I took a deep breath, smelling the fragrance of your perfume. For several stops, we sat side by side like that, thigh to thigh. I could feel your body trembling, and when I looked out the window, I saw our reflections in the glass. Saw that you had closed your eyes, that your face had a look that was close to perfect bliss.

You felt what I felt. I got that then. You felt as turned on by me as I was by you. After I saw that, I lifted your wrist and traced your pulse with my thumb. You shivered and opened your eyes, looking directly at me, and that was all the encouragement I needed.

Quickly, I took your hand and placed it against the huge bulge in my pants. Your eyes on mine grew wide and moist with want. You stroked my cock through the heavy denim. My back stiffened and I stifled a moan under a cough. We were still on public transit, remember. You didn't care. Casually, you slid your cardigan sweater off your shoulders and placed it over both of our laps. Beneath the soft mohair curls of the sweater, you unzipped my fly and reached your hand inside to feel my cock.

Bad girl, I thought. Such a dirty bad girl. Sensing what you need and going after it. I smiled as I felt your fingertips trip along my bone. Weren't we a pair? Too lost in the moment to care, to be discreet.

You sighed when you made the connection of flesh to flesh, running your fingers over my rod, then brushing against the skin of my belly as you did. Your touch sent a shiver through me. I almost came from that alone. I used my own hand to explore the crotch of your leather pants, not worrying about the horrified stares of the other passengers, not paying attention to anything but you until the bus driver screamed for us to leave, to get off before he called the cops. I was quick to oblige.

I pulled you through the doors after me, dragging you down the street to one of my favorite alleys. I was pleased to discover that you knew what I wanted you to do without me having to say a word. You put your hands flat against the brick wall in front of you and you let me undress you from behind. I pulled your leather jeans down your slender thighs, then slid your racy red panties down as well and began pawing at your pussy. I made your split even wetter with my spit before introducing you to my cock. You didn't moan as it went in, you simply steeled yourself, flexing your body like one long, hard muscle.

I pressed my lips against the back of your neck and said, "It's been years since I fucked someone."

"Make it last," you said back, your voice sounding pretty tough for someone in your position. Instead of making it last, I made this ride count, rocking my rod in and out of you like a well-greased piston, getting it all slippery wet with each forceful thrust. I worked you until you couldn't handle the wait, until you took one hand away from the bricks and brought it between your legs, teasing your clit, tugging on it with force.

I liked that. I must say, that I liked that a whole fucking lot. You were in control—even when you were out of control.

You kept your hand working between your legs, rotating in vibrant circles around your clit, and I kept driving inside of you until I felt myself build to climax. As I shuddered and started to moan, you let yourself reach it with me. We came together in a rush, your pussy contracting like a velvety fist around my prick. It was quick, but it was necessary. It did the job. I couldn't wait to do it again, slower, but I wanted to be in my own place for the sequel.

For a moment, you stayed in the position, your beautiful half-naked body exposed to the sunlight and the curious stares of anyone who walked past the mouth of the alley. It seemed as if you really needed time to contain yourself, to pull yourself back together. Then you slid your panties and leather slacks back up, and turned to face me as you did the zip and button.

"You *know*," you said, eyebrows raised. "You must know, right?"

"Know what?" I asked, gazing directly into your eyes.

"I got on the bus looking for you. My heart just stopped when I saw you sitting there—"

"You're kidding." I couldn't believe this.

"I've been riding it for a week."

Jesus, we'd probably been on different lines—different times—both of us cruising through the city, searching for strangers.

"I saw you before, saw the way you were looking at me. I couldn't get you out of my mind." You had your hand in mine now, and you were pulling me out to the street, hurrying me to our next carnal connection.

We didn't bother with the bus, this time.

We took a cab.

Operator 84

It's a long ride, as the crow flies, from Tribeca to the Upper West Side. But traffic's next to nothing at four in the morning—even on Saturday night.

We've been dancing in one of those exclusive Tribeca clubs—you know the one you like so much. You always get turned on when you're dancing. You always get really turned on. Maybe that's why you can't wait.

Or maybe it's because we've stumbled upon one of those rare New York fixtures—the female cab driver. Instead of grunting at us and talking about politics, traffic or the weather, she asks us in a musical voice: "Where can I take you?"

There's plenty of room in the back seat, but you snuggle up against me, your body lithe in its tight little black dress. You lean back and kiss me.

"Tenth and 77th," I tell the driver. Smiling, I add: "And make it snappy!"

"You've been reading too many detective novels," she says, smirking a little. She's somewhere in her mid-twenties, probably a student. She's got long blonde hair and pretty eyes, which she disguises with a Yankees cap pulled down indelicately over her face. "Been dancing?"

By then, you've started to snug up your black dress and reach under it. I look down at you with my eyes wide; I want to ask you what you're doing, but I sense instinctively, from knowing you so well, that nothing is going to stop you—so I may as well enjoy the ride.

"Yeah," I tell the driver. "We've been dancing."

Your lacy thong comes smoothly down your thighs, over your ankles. You kick off your flats and tuck your panties into the pocket of my dress slacks.

"Lots of great dancing down in Tribeca nowadays," says the cab driver, looking at me in the rear view mirror. I can see the side of her face and she's smiling; she's got a bright, enticing smile, and I spend about five seconds trying to figure out whether she knows what's going on. "Yup, the neighborhood's really bouncing back."

"Uh-huh," I say as you reach for my cock. "Bouncing."

By then you've slid down behind the seat and you're kneeling between my legs. Knowing better than to argue with you, of course, I spread them enough to give you access.

"Yeah," I say, my breath coming short as your hand closes around the rapidly-growing bulge in my pants. "There's nothing quite as great as a night dancing." I swallow nervously as you make short work of my belt and pants, apparently not carrying if the driver recognizes the telltale jingle of my belt buckle, the revealing sound of my zipper going down.

"Sure," she says. "Dancing's great. Getting all sweaty. All those bodies pressed in against yours...." She utters a girlish giggle, something I never expected to hear from a cab driver of any gender. "Meet anyone interesting?"

Your lips descend on my hard cock, sliding down effortlessly as your tongue works against the underside. I have a lot of difficulty speaking at this point, but I manage to carry on the conversation. "Oh, well, you know," I croak. "My wife and I....we weren't really there to meet people. Just to....dance."

"With each other," she says, turning to look at me and smile as the cab comes to a stop in traffic.

"Yeah," I say, as your mouth works its magic on my cock. "With each other."

"I can tell. Does your wife like dancing?"

My cock slips out of your mouth. "Oh yeah," you say from between my legs, slurping a little as you lick your lips. "I love to dance."

For a moment I'm afraid the cab driver's going to lean over the seat and look down, but she doesn't. Instead, she turns back around and hits the gas, giving your mouth on my cock a unique sort of gravity as you slowly pump my hardness in and out. I'm having trouble, now, struggling not to moan as the cab driver talks about how much she loves dancing.

"I love wearing something really sexy when I'm dancing," she says, glancing back to smile at me. "I can't dress sexy with my job, obviously. So I really like to doll up when I go to a club."

Now you've pulled my pants all the way down; they're around my ankles and your mouth is on my balls. "Oh really," I say, my throat tight with the effort of speaking. "What do you like to wear."

"Oh, you know, something like what your wife is wearing." She glances back again, her eyes dark with mystery. "Where'd she go, anyway?"

"Oh, I think she's asleep," I murmur. "She had a bit to drink at the club."

"I bet. I guess there's no reason to stop now."

My ears ring as I realize, without a doubt, that she knows what's going on. But both of us maintain the pretension, even as you take the hint and climb up into my lap—facing me.

"Yup, there's something very sexy about getting dressed up to go dancing," the cab driver says as you take my spit-slick cock in your hand and guide it to the entrance of your pussy. The cab driver looks back at us. "Oh, I'm sorry, am I distracting you?"

You moan softly as you settle down on top of me, my

cock deep inside you. You slump forward against me, heavily, and your hips start grinding in that way you do, barely moving but causing almost more friction than I can take. You know how to make me come—but, more importantly, you know how to make yourself come, and your hand is wedged tightly between our bodies, rubbing your clit.

"Of course, wearing something like what your wife is wearing, I can't wear much under it. I mean, when it's tight, you know, you get panty lines. I have to go with a little tiny thong. Do you find that, too?"

She glances over her shoulder, pretending not to notice that you're grinding on top of me, kissing me hard as you drive my cock rhythmically into your pussy.

"Yeah," you moan softly. "Sometimes I don't wear anything at all."

She giggles, turning back to the road. "Me, too," she says. "Of course, I didn't want to say that, but sometimes I just go with nothing on under my dress. Saves time later."

"Yeah," you say. "Oh God....saves time...."

I can tell you're going to come, and now we're clear of the midtown traffic, hurtling down Eighth Ave at a breakneck pace. It's almost like the cab driver is in competition with us, trying to see if she can get us where we're going before we can finish. But you're quick as a wink with that hand on your clit, and you don't try to camouflage your moans when you come. Your body presses hard against mine, your hips pumping rapidly, and you moan loudly, throwing back your head and whispering "Oh yes, oh yes, oh yes...."

Which is when I come, my hips working my cock up into you, your smooth thighs pressing against mine. I'm not quite as loud as you, but any hint that the cab driver is clueless is long since gone. I clutch you tight and kiss your neck as my orgasm dwindles.

When I open my eyes, I see that the driver is turned

around in her seat, her legs tucked under her. She's watching us—openly, shamelessly.

"Here we are," she says.

You slide off of me, my cock slipping out of you, wet and soft. I reach for my pants and start to pull them up, groping for my wallet as I do.

"How much do I owe you?" I ask, my face reddening.

"Oh, look at this," the driver says. "I forgot to turn on the meter. Well, we'll just call it even."

"Thanks," I say as you smile at her and get out of the cab.

"Operator eighty-four," she says, smiling as she hands me a card. "I work Fridays and Saturdays."

She smiles. She's taken off the Yankees cap, and I can see her pretty eyes flashing under the streetlights.

She turns back around and puts the cab in gear.

"Next time, though, don't expect the ride to be free."

I get out of the cab and hurry after you to the door of our apartment building.

The View from The Top

There were three of us there that night. Three hungry people who couldn't wait to dine. Not on some fantastic gourmet feast of food, but on each other. Yet although there was plenty of erotic heat warming the room, this was an unusual situation. In fact, I found myself absolutely charmed by the formality and the innocent nuances found in our living room. If this had gone down like the other love parties that I've been involved in, we would simply have gone at it. Just spread out on the floor and layered one body on another on another. A sticky pyramid of very sexy people. In the past, I've thought that nothing could top that. Now, I learned something new. Because you were shy, sort of embarrassed, incredibly unsure of yourself. You didn't know if you had it in you to try a menage.

That's not exactly true, is it? You knew you were capable, and you knew you wanted to, but you weren't jaded. You couldn't just leap, you had to slowly, carefully test the waters. You had to lower yourself in one millimeter at a time.

And this is how it happened—

We played a game. A reveal-all type of game. Each one of us told a secret we claimed we never had shared before. Audrey went first. I was surprised that she had any secrets left to share. The girl is an open book, and as her roommate for the past five years, I thought I knew everything. That's how fucking smug I was. But Audrey managed to surprise me right from the start. She looked at you, and she looked at me, and she said, "I was twenty-three before I popped my cherry."

Man, did that shock me. The girl has no boundaries now. She goes after what she wants and she generally gets it. Male or female. Friend or foe. When she saw my eyebrows raise, she just shrugged. "I waited for love," she said, "and it was fine. It was great. But it didn't actually last."

Next was my turn. I took a sip of my wine and I looked at you. I knew what I wanted to say. I wanted to say that you turned me on—but that was no fucking secret, was it? Really, I wanted to say more than that. That I liked you. I really liked you. But maybe you knew that, too. So what I ended up doing was telling the story about me and the girl I met online who turned out to be a guy. And Audrey, the wench, just could not stop laughing, because when I'd originally told her the story, I'd left out that more than minor detail.

"When did you figure it out?" she asked between giggles.

"None of your business," I told her, and that made you laugh, too. And at the sound of your voice, we both turned to look at you. Suddenly, the silence was heavy in the room. Because now, you were up to bat, and we waited, the two of us, like hungry lions. It was clear that we both wanted a chance with you. Audrey had been anticipating this day for as long as I had. We'd teased and flirted, gone bar-hopping and played footsie. Here it was. Ready to happen....

"I don't know how to—" you stopped, and then you looked down, and then you looked at Audrey. I waited, because what I wanted was for you to look at me. But you didn't.

"It's okay," Audrey said, softly. "We're all buddies here. Anything you say will stay within these walls."

"I don't know how to go down," you finished in a rush. So shy.

"Seriously?" That was Audrey again. She looks enraptured at the thought. Audrey is what I'd consider a pro.

"Seriously."

"I'll teach you," Audrey offered immediately. Your eyes got huge. What was she saying? Neither of us understood.

"I will," Audrey said, "That's what friends are for."

"But what do you mean?" you whispered.

"I'm going to teach you how to suck cock."

At her words, you looked over at your beautiful blonde best friend as if she'd completely lost her mind, then let your gaze wander down to the crotch of her chicly faded 501s. She caught the glance and knew exactly what you were thinking. "Not on me, silly," she explained, "on him."

She made a motion in my direction, and I immediately felt myself getting hard. I mean, harder. I'd been hard all night. I'd been ready all night. In my mind, the trio of us were already in that sticky pyramid I mentioned earlier. You on top and Audrey on the bottom. Or vice versa. Or me on top with the two of you below. Shifting and sliding in a sticky, sweaty groping fest. A perfect party where everyone got everything they'd ever wanted. And what I wanted was you.

Audrey had her hand on yours now, and she squeezed your fingertips, and then said, "Ready, baby?"

When you remained silent, she glanced at you, her startling green eyes opened wide. "You *do* like my roommate, don't you?"

Now, you blushed, and I loved you for it. How many innocents are there left in L.A.? Three? And you were definitely one of them. And the prettiest, sexiest one that I'd ever seen. I waited anxiously to hear your answer. *Did* you like me? Didn't you? I thought you did, from the way you flirted with me at the last holiday party that Audrey and I held at our little bungalow. From the way you always seemed to want to hang out in my room, even though Audrey is your close friend. If you didn't like me, why would you sprawl on my bed and talk to me about any subject? Why would you make it your business to know mine?

Maybe you never knew that I had a crush on you—you see me with my dates, different starlets, different movie people, but you know what? You're the one I think is the hottest.

"Why not start me off with a banana?" you asked, twirling one caramel-colored curl around your fingertips.

"Bananas break," Audrey said knowingly. "You don't want to choke. If anything, we can use a cucumber to get you ready for the main event—"

Before you could say a word, Audrey headed to the kitchen. It was just you and me in the living room, and I could tell that you wanted to look at me, to talk to me, but you just played with your hair, and then stared at your hands. See, baby, I knew everything. I knew that you and Audrey had talked threesomes a lot, that you were the one to bring it up in the first place. Naive, yes. But you have had those desires for a long time, haven't you? And you knew that you'd be safe with us.

We heard her rustling around in the refrigerator, and when she came back, she had a slender zucchini in one hand. "We were all out of cukes. So this will have to do." You sat staring at the vegetable and then you started to laugh. The whole charade was so ridiculous. You wanted to go down on me, and I wanted to go down on you, and yet you had a zucchini in your lap. What the fuck was up with that?

"Here's the deal," Audrey began. "Breathing is the most important part of going down deep. Before you slide the zucchini into your throat, I want you to exhale—"

Her instructions reminded me of the yoga tape she works out to. *Don't breathe the breath, let the breath breathe you.* Still, even in this ludicrous situation, you did your best, drawing the head into your mouth. I stifled a groan as I watched you work the slippery zucchini further in. Never felt jealous of a vegetable before, but I guess there's a first time for everything.

Audrey acted as if she were oblivious of the fact that I was even in the room, continuing in her X-rated instructions, "Inhale when you pull it out, and you'll be ready for him to slide inside you again."

At her words, you pushed the smooth veggie-tool back into your throat, and I watched as you tentatively tried swallowing down on it. Quickly, you pulled the zucchini back out again.

"It feels weird," you said.

"You need the real thing," Audrey assured you. "But don't worry, I'll never leave your side. What you require in this sort of situation is an oral authority." You stared down at the slippery zucchini discarded despondently in your lap. "Giving head is just like anything else," Audrey continued. "You learn the little tricks of the trade, and your confidence grows. You know he'll be gentle with you. Just keep your hand on the base of his cock, and you'll be in control. You can push back if he's going too fast."

"Sure," I said, happy to at last be part of the conversation. "We'll go at your pace."

Your face was as purely crimson as your dress, and no matter what I said, you couldn't meet my eyes. I just smiled as Audrey perched her lithe body up on the arm of my chair and started whispering to me. I'm sure that you could make out snippets of her discussion— "Not a virgin, just not super comfortable with the whole idea" —and then you looked down at your hands again.

After a moment, I came to sit by your side. "Is it something you really want to learn?" I asked.

You nodded.

"Then it's best to practice with friends," and the Cheshire grin on my face let you know I understood precisely how ridiculous this all was. A willing nymphet was going to give me a blow job. In plainer English, a girl that I really, really liked was going to put her pretty, rose-slicked mouth around my rock-hard cock. On top of that, I would be expected to give instructions all the way through. "But I'd like it if Audrey would help you relax, first," I said, and as I spoke, your naughty best friend got into position on the floor between your thighs and lifted the hem of your dress. Doesn't Audrey always know what to do? Now, she was going to relax you with a little mouth-to-pussy while you got ready to learn how to give head.

As soon as you felt Audrey's warm breath on your panties, you sighed. As soon as you sighed, I put your hand on the crotch of my jeans. We were starting from the top. Slowly, you worked down my button fly. Then I watched as you split the jeans open for me, revealing the masterful tower of my erection. I'm not bragging here. The thing *was* masterful. I'd been hard now for longer than I could take. Just the thought of your sweet lips around my tool made me want to shoot. So when your hands fumbled with the crotch of my jeans, well, I must say that I'd never been bigger than that before.

Audrey had her mouth pressed against your pussy now through your panties. That was obvious from the way your cheeks had flushed even pinker and your eyes held the warmest, sweetest glow. You were definitely relaxing now. Pleasure like this couldn't be bad, right? That's what you seemed to be thinking. And with a quick little sigh, you turned your head and opened your gorgeous mouth, bringing the tip of my hard-on between your lips.

Wetness. That was the instant sensation I felt. Lovely, perfect wetness. Warm wetness. Oh, for a novice, you really knew what you were doing. Or maybe you weren't such a novice after all— The concept bloomed in my head as you licked your tongue in a line up the length of my shaft. Could you have been playing us this whole time? Pretending to be sweet and shy and naive, when really you knew exactly what you were doing? I didn't have the time or the inclination to ask. I simply praised your technique.

"That's the way," I said, sliding my hands through your light brown curls. "You just relax and take it all the way down. The key word here is relax, and remember to breathe—"

You swallowed against the skin of my cock, then drew the length further down your throat. As you worked me harder, Audrey continued her kissing and licking games between your legs. I could hear her making subtle, slurping noises, and I knew how excited you were getting, because you started to kiss me in an even more energetic, enthusiastic fashion. You swirled your tongue around the shaft of my cock, then closed your lips firmly on the head, sucking hard.

"You like what Audrey's doing?" I murmured to you, and you stopped working me just long enough to moan in assent. The sound vibrated around me, and I had to grip onto your shoulders to steady myself. I would have come right then if I had less control. But I made myself wait. I knew things were just going to continue to get better and better and better.

As Audrey continued to play dirty tricks with the tip of her tongue around your clit, you did the same thing to the head of my cock. I figured that out right away. You were mimicking her strokes, and I thanked Audrey silently for the gift she was bestowing upon both of us. When she brought her hands into the action, cradling your hips and lifting up, you slid one hand down to gently cup and stroke my balls.

"Oh, yeah," I moaned, "just lightly. Just like that."

You continued as I requested, so I continued to talk. "Maybe just graze your nails against them," I said, and immediately you made that wish come true. Your touch was magical, light and perfect, and I started to thrust into your mouth. But you wanted to take things slowly, so you did as

Audrey had said. You put your hands on my thighs, holding me back. We were going at your pace, and I had to force myself to play by your rules.

But now, as Audrey continued to dine on you, I brought one hand against your throat and stroked there. "Relax," I said. "Relax and just let it happen. If you need to pull back for a second, that's okay."

At my instructions, you opened up and I felt my cock slip a little further down your throat. Unable to help myself, I sped up the rhythm now, sliding back and forth, gaining a bit of headroom with each thrust. It was as if I were fucking all the way through you, and I must say that the thought turned me on even more. The three of us were in serious motion. Constant motion. I could hear the licking and sucking noises as Audrey really worked you fiercely. As I grew more aroused, I groaned out loud. You responded immediately, your fingers tripping down behind my balls, caressing that transforming spot back there, dancing the tips of your fingers more firmly against my skin.

How'd you learn that trick? Huh, baby? How'd you learn just where to touch? Once again, I thought that you were more experienced than you let on, but that was fine with me. If you wanted to choose a role, if that would make you happy, well I was more than willing to be an actor in your play.

I continued to help you now, so close to reaching the climax, thrusting deeper and deeper into your throat. You had to move to get more comfortable, and you pulled away from Audrey and went on all fours on the sofa, facing me, drinking me.

Immediately, Audrey got behind you on the sofa, and I watched in the mirror on the opposite wall as she slid your panties all the way down your thighs and off, and then squirmed her way back into a position that allowed her to dine from your pussy once again. And as she brought you right to the peak, I started to come. My moans grew louder, my breathing harsher. I gripped my hands onto your shoulders, held tight, and shot my load deep down your throat. You swallowed against me, draining every last drop, and then slowly I slid from your lips and collapsed back against the sofa.

Pulling away from Audrey, you sprawled next to me. When you flicked your tongue over your top lip, I could have come again. It was as if you were savoring my taste, and I just can't imagine any other action looking sexier.

"See?" I murmured, reaching out to stroke your hair out of your eyes. "Now, you're an oral authority as well."

You looked at me, then looked over at our green-eyed friend, whose mouth was shiny with your own erotic juices. "Time to share the pleasure," you told me, as we both reached for Audrey and spread her out on the couch....

But now, little miss I-don't-know-how-to-go-down, you had plans of your own. Now, feeling cocky, you were in total control. You had Audrey spread her thighs and you went immediately between them, sucking against the swollen bud of her clit. Licking in long, lush strokes between her nether lips. You were ferocious and hungry, and I sat back on the sofa and watched you work her.

Audrey seemed stunned. She had gotten excited from making you come, but it was clear from the expression on her face that she hadn't expected you to return the favor, at least not so quickly and not so well. I could have told her otherwise. I'd just had the most amazing experience in your hands, or really your mouth, so I could have told Audrey all about what was waiting for her. Instead, I staked my place close by and watched.

What a pretty picture the two of you made. Audrey was in instant ecstasy. Her blonde hair framed her face and her lips formed a perfect 'o' as she felt your tongue slide inside her. You were intent on bringing her pleasure. You had your hands around her hips, and then slowly you worked your fingers down, until you held open the lips of her pussy. I could see the shiny wetness on your lips, and I could see your tongue flickering back and forth over Audrey's clit. I knew she was going to come soon, and suddenly, I couldn't wait to be part of the action again.

Moving quickly, I got behind you and lifted your dress in back. Your lovely ass was there, waiting, and I stroked you once, softly, to let you know my plans. The groan you made against Audrey's skin told me you were ready. Gently, I parted your thighs from behind and slid inside you. My cock was still wet from your mouth, and now that wetness met and mingled with the moisture inside your pussy. My god, were you turned on. And how wet you were only fueled the way I felt. My rig was so hard and ready. I slid it in deep and made you moan again.

Audrey seemed to like that. Each time you made a noise against her pussy, she mirrored your sighs and groans and moans herself. I could tell that she was into the reverberating feelings of your voice echoing within her. It was more than my delight to help my roommate reach her peak by making you continue to moan steadily against her pussy. I liked that thought. Gripping into your long hair, I held you firmly as I worked you. My cock stroked in deep, and then slid back out, then in again, until we were sealed together, and then slowly out, leaving only the head inside you.

"Oh, yes," you said now, dragging out the word, "yessss," and Audrey whispered the same word along with you. The three of us were so finely joined together, that I sensed it when Audrey started to come. I slid one hand under your body, strumming your clit as my pleasure built. And soon the three of us were coming together—teasing each other onward with our voices and our bodies until there was no higher level to be reached.

We'd already hit the top.

Couch Surfing

I've been sleeping on the couch ever since she and I broke up. It's been two full months; I counted our anniversary and celebrated on the couch with a private glass of her best cognac.

I tried couch surfing for a week or two, but friends in their late twenties seem to need their space more than ones in the first quarter-century of life. I ran out of places to stay, and she invited me back, showing obvious pleasure at the fact that I'd come crawling back to her. All my stuff was still in the apartment, so she felt obliged to put complex and somewhat unpredictable limits on my use of "her bedroom," the bedroom we shared for several years. Eventually, I learned to just stay the hell out of there.

Not good enough.

About two weeks ago, she decided she "needed her space" and moved all my stuff into the living room in big piles and milk crates. I'm supposed to be looking for an apartment, but it's a tough market...and I suppose I don't really want to leave yet.

That pleases her. She imagines I'm hoping we'll get back together. She thinks I'm still hung up on her.

But I'm not—that's not what's going on at all.

You and she weren't really friends, just college acquaintances who bumped in to each other on the street when she needed someone else to fill the streetside bedroom in the big Victorian.

I hate to admit it, but I've had a crush on you since shortly after she and I started to get bored with each other. I used to chat with you after she went to bed, when you were sitting up having a cup of herbal tea or whatever, reading the paper, wearing a tank top and gym shorts. I used to find excuses to talk with you about your work, your classes, your background. I even managed to sneak in a few questions about your boyfriends, to razz you about the guys you brought home those three times, never letting them make more than brief guest appearances in your bed. Brief guest appearances, that figured prominently in my fantasies.

You haven't dated a lot, something I find absolutely bewildering. It shocks me that you don't have guys following you around, begging you for dates. You're pretty, unquestionably, and you've got a body that I could never take my eyes off when we would sit there and talk, your tank top thin and damp with sweat, clinging to the curves of your slight breasts, your gym shorts a little too snug to properly hide the contours of your body. But you're shy, I guess, so you're single, and you've been that way for most of your adult life, with only a few scattered relationships here and there. I find it hard to believe, but you haven't been gobbled up yet.

I wanted to gobble you up, even then. It wasn't the problems I was having with her that made me want that; I'd noticed you the first time she'd introduced us, and had a lot of trouble taking my eyes off of you. I used to catch surreptitious glances of you around the apartment, used to feel my pulse race when I saw that you'd left the bathroom door ajar while you were showering—that finicky door that never closes right. The shower has a clear glass door, and I used to want so badly to push the door open and look at you, drink in your glorious, slender body.

But it's tough, when you've got a girlfriend like she is. She would have been insanely jealous even if she didn't have a hot roommate. She used to give me shit about girls I didn't even like, ones who wouldn't have turned my head if they'd been on fire. She used to ask me if I found them attractive, if I thought they were prettier than she was, whether I wanted to fuck them. I always told her "No, no, no," and I learned to drop my gaze, not to look around when we were out together. I learned to tell her I didn't want to fuck any of the women we saw on the street, any of her other friends. I used to tell her I didn't find any of them the least bit attractive. Lies, occasionally, but then I learned to believe them myself, I suppose.

She never asked about you. I don't know what I would have said. I think she's really that clueless; she thinks of you as her mousy roommate, incapable of competing with her in the arena of love. Maybe I'm being uncharitable because I'm surrounded by the stuff she dumped in the living room— but I really think she's that oblivious.

She never noticed the way I looked at you, or didn't look at you, when she was around. She never noticed the way I'd drop my gaze, avert my eyes from your breasts when you were wearing something tight, the way I'd get flustered when you unexpectedly darted across the living room wrapped in a skimpy towel. The way I'd work extra hard to seem casual when we were all chatting, being the magnanimous, friendly boyfriend, never admitting I'd rather be talking to you than her.

Now, that's all gone. There's no illusion of monogamy to be kept. There's only the dissolving need for propriety, the vanishing hunger to do the right thing. And it's getting so I don't care any more.

Which scares me, because she sleeps right next to you, on the other side of a wall so thin I know you must have listened to us. I know you must have heard every detail, because I listened to you, the few times you brought home guys. I listened to you, fascinated, trying desperately not to get hard as she and I lay there inert, her mumbling uncharitable comments about you being an inconsiderate slut, a bitch who cared more about your pleasure than about whether your roommates could get a good night's sleep.

She really said that, I'm afraid. I just shrugged and closed my eyes, knowing if I reached out to touch her, if I kissed her, if I got hard and made love to her while your anonymous boy was making love to you, she'd catch on that it made me hot, listening to you. She'd catch on that I was cataloguing every sound from your lips, every creak of the bedsprings, every slam of the headboard against her wall. I was listening to the sound of fervent thrusting, listening to you moan, louder than she'd ever moaned, sounds verging on a sob as you said "I'm coming" so loud that she and I could hear it. Then listening to the rising pitch of your desperate cries, orgasms that sounded so intense it almost hurt me to listen, mingled with her disgusted scoffs as she said "yuck" and shook her head.

I barely heard her, because I was listening so intently, picturing you under your nameless lover or atop him, fucking him ardently. I was picturing the posture of your body as you thrust your nude body against him, mentally imagining the look on your face as you came. Building the orgasm that exploded through your body as he slid rhythmically into you.

And wondering if I could make you come, too.

"I'm going to sleep," I told her, and rolled over onto my belly, hiding my cock as it swelled.

The layout of this old Victorian is kind of strange, in some ways. The front bedroom is on the opposite side of the living room from the only bathroom. You always get up early in the morning to use it. I always pretend to be asleep.

You sleep nude; I know that. Even in the cold, which is probably why you always seem to leave the heater on. I don't know it for a fact, but I glimpsed you once, shortly after you moved in, on a December midnight when the door to your bedroom, swollen with winter, drifted open. You were sprawled on your bed, the heater blasting, heat pouring out of your bedroom and into the living room, so intense I could feel it. There, in the dry half-darkness, you lay naked on top of your sheets, glistening with sweat. The sheets tangled just beneath your hips, just barely hiding the crack of your slender ass from me. The curve of your hips fascinated me, and my eyes ran all over you. You were face down, and I couldn't see your breasts—just the violin curve of your back and shoulders, the abandon of your arms shoved up over your head, the curious posture of your ass, thrust slightly out and slightly up under the sweat-damp sheet as its contours clung to the shape of you.

Your legs were slightly spread.

My breath came quick and hard as I imagined that posture to be a position of invitation, and I felt my cock getting hard. I wanted to slip into your bedroom, close that quarrelsome door, and delicately tug the sheet away from your body. It almost hurt to think of looking at your pussy, exposed between your spread thighs, beneath the welcoming curve of your ass. It *did* hurt to think about wriggling my face beneath you, molding my mouth to your pussy, and devouring you, making you moan and come until you could only beg me to enter you, lifting your ass in the air and inviting me in.

It hurt so bad my hands shook, as I pulled the door closed as quietly as I could, and went back to bed.

The door creaked as I pulled it, and I saw you jerk and stir. You sat up, and your dark hair swayed as you turned your head.

"What?" I heard you say.

"The door came open," I called.

"Oh," you said sleepily. "Yeah. I've got to fix it."

I didn't know whether to pray that you would, or you wouldn't. My cock, hardening, wanted it one way. My girlfriend wanted it the other.

When you get up in the morning you walk sleepily to the bathroom, lingering longer in the living room than you would if I wasn't pretending to be asleep. Watching through slitted lids, I see your ass as you stretch your arms over your head, the bottom of your T-shirt lifting so I can see your white panties, see the way they cling to your pert ass. It's gotten so I anticipate that moment, every morning, laying on the couch longer than I would otherwise, since I can't sleep well with all the traffic noise. I lay there, watching you stretch, looking at your body, longing for the moment when you turn around. Your nipples show through the well-worn T-shirts you wear; I wish I could open my eyes and see them more clearly. Instead, I admire them through the dim curtain of my eyelashes as I fake slow, somnolent breathing.

Usually you just stretch, walk into the bathroom and get in the shower. It's not until ten minutes later when I get my next look, you in a towel wrapped damp around your body, clutching it just above your nipples, your legs scissoring as you walk across the living room, unaware that I'm watching them, drinking them in, wondering what they'd feel like spread around my face, my thighs, my hips.

But sometimes, it doesn't go like that.

It's happened more than once, that's what scares me. Twice while you were standing there in a T-shirt and panties, thinking I was sleeping. Twice when you were shrouded in a towel, your dark hair dripping on the hardwood floor.

And once when you caught me with my eyes open, when you knew, without a doubt that I was looking.

You stood there and stared at me. You watched me

sleeping, watched the faked rise and fall of my sleeping chest. Your eyes ran up and down my body, caressed my face.

And that one time, when you realized my eyes were open, you looked right at me.

And you smiled.

I never asked you about that moment. Did you know how bad I was wanting you? It's utterly beyond me how it could escape you, because you're the most gorgeous thing in the world. I can't imagine any man seeing you *without* wanting you.

But we never talked about it. That was a week ago, and I've been slipping since then, my longing looks catching you as we chat after she's gone to bed, before she's gotten up, while she's out with her friends, dancing, "spreading her wings," as she says. I've been slipping, standing outside your door, trying to will the swollen door to pop open and show me your body, stretched nude on the bed, face up, legs spread, eyes open, lips parted, arms over your head, back arched and breasts upthrust, beckoning me. I've been slipping, my cock growing hard as I listened to you shower, imagining the hot water caressing your naked body the way I want to caress it.

She doesn't notice. I'm quite sure it's not that she doesn't care, because the nasty comments she makes tell me she'd still freak if I found another woman attractive. She manages to ignore it, though, probably because she never looks at me, and manages to make herself conspicuously absent most of the times I'm home. She rarely says anything to me, and when I am home, she seems bound and determined to parade around me in her underwear, sometimes with breasts bare, showing that casual disregard for nudity that comes in a long relationship—but that feels so strange, now. She tries to make it clear that she doesn't care if I look, but it seems like she does care—that she wants to look, wants to torture me. She gets huffy when I avert my eyes as she stands there talking to me, barely clad. Other times, she doesn't talk to me at all, reducing our interactions to monosyllabic grunts.

She still talks to you, though. She talks to you like you're her sister, and the two of you have been friendly the whole time she and I have been breaking up. She invites you out dancing with her and her friends, supposing, it seems, that you've also got wings that need spreading. You always turn her down. I've overheard her telling you about the other guys she's started seeing, casual things, progressing quickly to sex that, I heard as I eavesdropped once, makes me look like "A seventy-year-old man who lost his Viagra."

Strangely, though, it didn't hurt my feelings that she would describe me uncharitably. It didn't make me jealous that she was fucking other guys already, meeting them in bars and clubs while she was spreading her wings, celebrating being free of me. It didn't piss me off that she was bragging to you about what a crappy lover I was, making spiteful remarks about the size of my equipment. That didn't bother me at all.

What bothered me was that when you saw me next, your face flushed red and you looked down, almost unable to speak to me. What bothered me is that you might have believed it. Not because I care what anyone thinks of me.

But because it might make you not want to fuck me. Not that I *would* fuck you, of course—that would be out of the question, unwholesome, inconsiderate of her feelings. Sleeping with random strangers met in bars is one thing, but fucking her roommate? Impossible.

Which is hardly the point. Because it's not that I want you to fuck me, or consider it a possibility.

I just want *you* to want it.

And I spend a lot of time wondering if you do.

*****

I'm ashamed that I did it, because it seems so invasive. I never would have done something like this before, but I was alone and hurting, finding myself wondering, crazy, where you were. Were you out flirting with someone? Were you going to bring him home and fuck him where I could hear?

I wandered into your room. I could smell you, that unique scent that everyone has, like a signature. It intoxicated me. Or maybe I want to find an excuse.

I bent low over your bed. I inhaled your essence, running my fingertips over the place where your naked body had been, where it had left its impression. I touched the sheets, knowing they'd caressed your body.

Your vibrator was tucked underneath the sheets, its long wand and bulbous head hidden deep inside your bed. I pulled it out and looked at it, breathing hard. I imagined you sprawled on your back, spread, pressing the head of the vibrator to your clit as your hips worked in double-time, your naked body writhing, your face twisted in concentration and rapture as you approached your orgasm.

I lifted it to my face and breathed.

It smelled like you. Like a you I'd never smelled before.

It smelled like your pussy.

My hands shaking, I tucked the vibrator back under your sheets, not even able to take the time to make sure it was in the same position you left it. I wasn't even sure I knew.

I left your room fast, and tried not to remember that scent. But it kept showing up in my mind, filling my nostrils, intoxicating me. Especially when I'd lay there, eyes slitted, and watch you walk across the living room.

It's Saturday night. She's out again, out with friends. You're in your room with the door closed, talking on the phone. I'm in the living room, propped on my couch, the couch that's become my home. I'm watching television and listening to your voice, seeming musical, distant, beneath the sound of the TV.

You come out of your bedroom wearing a short T-shirt and tight black shorts. I try not to look at you. You walk across the living room, giggling "Sorry" and dancing on tiptoes as you dart across my field of vision, in front of the television. I smile and nod. You look back at me, pausing from the door of the bathroom. I smile some more. You smile back. I think, for a moment, that I see you blush.

My cock aches. I look at the closed bathroom door and imagine you in there, bent over the sink as you wash your face. I wonder if you're wearing anything under your shorts. It didn't look like it, from the brief glimpse I got. I remember the scent on your vibrator, and my cock hurts more.

You come out of the bathroom. Your T-shirt is tight, your nipples evident underneath, capping your small breasts. You're not wearing a bra. My eyes flicker over the outline of your upper body, of your smooth belly underneath the hem of your short T-shirt. I can see the contours of your crotch through the tight shorts. You're barefoot, and even your feet turn me on.

You walk over to the couch and sit down next to me.

"What's on?" you ask.

"Not much," I say, channel surfing.

"Just vegging out?"

"Yeah," I say.

"She's cute," you say.

"Huh? Who?"

"That actress. What's her name?"

I turn, look at you. God, you look gorgeous. You brush your dark hair out of your eyes and smile. You lick your lips, those slim lips I've so often wanted to kiss.

"I don't know," I tell you.

We stare at the TV, vegging out together. You're close enough that I can smell you, the scent I recognized in your room that time, and it kills me to know that lurking somewhere underneath it is the smell I found on your vibrator. I breathe deeply. You stare straight ahead. I try to do the same, but it's not working very well. I keep glancing at you, watching your pretty face in the flickering light of the TV.

"You two used to watch porn together," you say.

My ears pop. My chest gets tight.

"Um," I say. "Yeah, occasionally."

"I watched that one you rented."

"Which one?"

"Forbidden something."

I take a deep breath, trying very hard not to look at you— and succeeding, this time. I feel my face getting hot. Really hot.

"Did you like it?"

"Yeah," you say. "A lot."

I feel a stab of nervousness in my gut. "Did you watch it alone?"

"Maybe," you say.

"You watched it with a guy, didn't you?"

"You know what I liked the most? The scene where she did her roommate. That was hot."

You turn toward me, the vaguest hint of a smile on your face. My cock's fully hard, now, my breath coming quick as I look at you.

"I don't remember that one," I tell you.

"Hmm," you say. "Maybe I can show you how it goes."

And that's it, for a minute. It just hangs there in the air, my cheeks sizzling, you staring at the TV.

"So how 'bout it?" you ask.

"Um," I say. "How about what?"

"You know."

I think about it for a minute.

"She'd be upset," I say.

You laugh. "Um, yeah," you say.

"Still," I say stupidly. "It's tempting."

I can't believe we're actually discussing this. You're throwing yourself at me, and I'm talking about it instead of doing it. I look at you, scared, all my lust for you vanished in the pounding of my heart and the guilt that flows through me.

You smile.

"Fuck it," I say, and come for you.

Your mouth tastes like vodka, and I feel foolish not to have noticed you're a little drunk. Then that's gone, too, and there's only the feel of your tongue against mine, the press of your body as I push you back onto the couch. Your lips part and we kiss, my arms going around you as you moan in surprise. You feel my hard-on touch your thigh and you grind against it, your hands sliding down to the small of my back and pulling me more firmly onto you.

"Don't you care that she'll be pissed?" you whisper when I start kissing your throat.

"No," I lie, and trace my fingertips over your stomach.

Your body feels incredible against mine; your smell fills my nostrils. We kiss for a long time, squirming and writhing on the couch. The TV plays on unwatched until I feel your hands sliding down the back of my sweats.

I reach out, find the remote control, kill the television. You start to slide my sweats off.

My cock comes free, hard and bouncing. You push me onto my back and slide down my body, zeroing in on my cock like you've wanted it forever. Your lips close around my head and you suck it into your mouth, your tongue stroking the underside of my shaft. I moan, looking down at your pretty face as you suck me. Your hands travel up my body, caressing my chest as you swallow me whole.

When you come up for air, you look at me, your lips glistening, your breath quick.

"Let's go into my bedroom," you say.

I have to pull my sweats up to be able to walk. You take my hand and lead you into your room, as if I wouldn't go there of my own volition.

We close the door, and I press it hard to make sure it doesn't come open. We stand there, awkwardly, looking at each other.

Then your arms cross, you take hold of your shirt, and it comes off you in one smooth movement, sailing into the corner. I stand, staring at your breasts, transfixed.

Then I reach for my own clothes and quickly tear off my sweats and T-shirt. You wriggle out of your shorts and we look at each other nude. Your eyes roam up and down my body. My cock stands straight out, pointing at you.

The touch of our naked bodies together seems the first time I really know it's going to happen, and it sends a pulse through my body. I bear you back onto the bed, smelling you on your sheets as I kiss your breasts and lick my way down your belly. You spread your legs wide, your smooth thighs seeming so familiar from the many times I've looked at them. I lick my way to your pussy and taste you, powerful and delicious. You moan as my tongue swirls around your lips, presses into your entrance, then moves up to your clit. When I lick that, hard, you do more than moan. Your hips rise to meet me, grinding your cunt against my face, quaking as you grasp the top of my head. I keep licking, hungrily, wanting more of you with every taste. My hands come to rest on your tits, fondling your hard nipples with my palms. I ride you as you buck and thrust against me. Your coarse, short hair tickles my nose. I press in harder and lick deeper, bringing louder moans from your parted lips.

"Fuck me," you say.

I lick my way back up to your mouth, kissing you, feeling you tongue me hungrily, tasting yourself. You arch your back and push up against me, beckoning my cock into you. You guide it with your hand, and when it touches your pussy, you slide it smoothly between the lips. I enter you, feeling your body stiffen as your tightness embraces me. I realize how wet you are, how loud you're moaning, how hard your fingers are digging into the flesh of my buttocks. You pull me firmly against you, whispering "You feel good" in my ear as the hard peaks of your nipples press against my chest.

I start to fuck you, slowly at first, then matching your rhythm as you thrust up onto me. Your pussy feels strange, familiar yet new, almost uncomfortably tight. It feels like you're clenching your muscles, trying to embrace me tighter, seeking to milk out all the pressure my cock has to offer. I fuck you faster and your hips match me, pumping in time as I pant in your ear. You're smooth, at first, the movements of your body telling me you just want to fuck me, you don't want to come. And I don't care, at first, because it feels so fucking good to be sliding into you. But then your whimpers get lower in pitch, the thrusts of your hips more insistent, the press of your body more solid against mine, your whispering moans of "fuck me, fuck me" more demanding. You're getting closer. I sense the curve of your pussy and grind my hips in a slow circle, pressing up against the sides of your pussy. That brings a long, low moan from your open mouth, your breath warm and wet against my ear as you rub your upper body against mine. Your breasts are magnificent, and I bend low to suckle them as I fuck you. That's when you gasp, grab my hair, and beg me not to stop.

You're close, now, very close. I had no idea your nipples were so sensitive; the feel of your body lunging and squirming underneath me as I lick them makes my mind flood with all the memories of you wearing tight shirts with no bra, thin undershirts on your way to the bathroom. Then it hits me that I'm inside you, I'm fucking that pussy I've so admired, sliding between those thighs I've wanted, forever, to spread. I realize that tucked into my hands are the firm cheeks I've watched so many times in tight shorts, bending over, or through slitted lids in panties. I squeeze your ass tightly and pound into you harder, my mouth molded to one of your nipples as you stop begging and start howling for me not to stop.

And that's how it happens. Easy as that, like the movies. My cock pulses as I feel the muscles of your pussy contract, and there's that frozen moment of silence before you cry out, just as I come, our orgasms mingling as we come together.

When we grind to a halt, panting, exhausted, it all dissolves and I stroke your hair, breathing your scent.

"She's really going to be pissed," you say.

"Fuck it," I tell you, and start kissing your breasts again.

It's after midnight when I open the door to your room, naked, drunk with long hours of fucking, my cock moist with your pussy.

She's there, in the living room, sitting on the couch, staring at me with fury in her face. She's wearing her little black dress and her high heels, and her arms are crossed over her breasts.

She doesn't say a word, just stares.

I just stare back for a long time, and then I sigh sadly, shaking my head.

She looks away.

I guess it's back to couch surfing, I think. *And not just for me.*

I close the bedroom door and come back to bed.

Birthday Queen

You invited the four of us to take you out for your birthday to one of the most expensive restaurants in the city. What a subtle trick that was, to choose your own setting, create your own party, and not have to pay for a thing. Maybe some people would have considered it crass, but I didn't really mind, since I'd always wanted to see the inside of the dome-like trattoria. Yet I grew less keen on the idea as the evening progressed.

We go way back, you and me, since high school. Maybe that's why I've always been a little indulgent with you. I know your past, all about you. Your secrets. I've seen you at your best and at your worst. Usually, everything evens out. But on this night, I guess you really decided you wanted to be Birthday Queen, and we were cast as your humble servants. You ordered the most expensive champagne on the menu and continued to down glass after glass while the rest of us watched you in a sort of dumbstruck awe. Look, that's part of your charm. You're always outspoken, which probably has something to do with your chosen profession. As a lawyer you need plenty of confidence, but drunk...your cockiness took on a nightmarish quality. With your curls high on your head and your blue eyes glistening, you looked like an angel in the reproduction that hung on the wall behind you. But your tongue was purely influenced by the devil, for you proceeded to tell each one of us our shortcomings.

The other three, also drinking, though not as quickly as you, were slightly numbed to your harsh words. I, as the designated driver, committed the tirade to memory. The evening was long and unenjoyable. When it was over, I drove my friends home, keeping you, well-buckled and passed-out, with me.

In the morning, you found yourself in my bed. Tied down to my bed. Your bleary eyes must have been startled when you opened them at half-past ten. You were on my satin sheets, on your stomach, completely naked. Cautiously, you turned your head on the pillow as I walked into the room.

"What...?" you started, tensing your arms, trying to get them free from the bindings. That wouldn't work. I'm fairly adept with a knot.

"Your birthday's over, baby," I said sweetly, "but I didn't get a chance to give you a birthday spanking yesterday. And let me tell you, I would have liked to. Oh, yeah—" I grinned at you, to show that although I wasn't kidding, I saw plenty of humor in this situation. "I would have liked to put you right over my lap at City Restaurant. To slide your sweet skirt up past your hips and spank that gorgeous ass of yours. And if you'd kept on going in the vein you were in, I definitely would have."

You closed your eyes and then opened them again, obviously trying to figure out if you were having a dream, or an alcohol-inspired hallucination. When you couldn't wake yourself up, you whispered, "You're not serious."

I showed you the paddle in my hand, brought it very close to your face so you could really see it. I must admit now, I'd been saving the paddle for just the right time. Now, was the time. "You behaved like a spoiled brat last night, and we had to pay for it. This morning, you're going to pay for it, with your skin."

You swallowed hard and tried to get a sweet, loving expression on your face. You turned your lips up hopefully and said, "But, honestly, you must be joking. You must..."

Hey, I know you. We've had our tumbles on sheet-strewn

mattresses before. That time in Mexico. That morning on the beach in Santa Monica. You and I fit together. So I took the time to place one hand between the split of your legs and saw just how wet you were. So wet, baby doll. That told me everything I needed to know.

"Ready?" I asked, giving you an out. If you screamed or told me to untie you immediately, I would have. But you didn't, did you? You got a cute little blush on your face and you lowered your chin and nodded.

"Then say it."

"Ready—" you whispered.

I gave you the first blow, then, catching both of your asscheeks, leaving a red blush-like print on your pale skin. You were tan elsewhere, but I'd spanked you where your bathing suit covered. You gasped at the sensation and then your eyes flashed fiercely as you tried to contain yourself. You knew that your tongue had gotten you in trouble already. If you said something indiscreet now, I might go harder on you still.

"You're twenty-eight, now," I said, matter-of-factly. "That was one. You have twenty-seven to go."

Now, still tensing your arm muscles, you started to realize I meant business. I gave you two more quick spanks, one on each cheek, to let you know you were right. I wasn't kidding. Then, going on one knee on the bed, I let the spanking continue, raining blows on your left cheek, then your right, heating you up in the most delicious and delectable manner. I paused when I saw the tears on your cheeks. I liked them. You murmured, much more humble, "Was I really a bitch last night?"

"Keep thinking," I said, "It'll all come back to you."

You closed your eyes as I gave you the last of the blows, and your breath was coming harder when I'd finished. "Twenty-eight," I said, standing by your side, placing one hand on your ass to feel the warmth. You sighed at my touch, and I let my fingers wander down again, between your asscheeks, to your pussy, which was (as I'd suspected it would be) even more drippingly wet than before. The clear sheen of your pleasure had decorated your inner thighs.

"I was... I was awful last night," you confessed, wiping your face on my pillow, "Wasn't I?"

"Slightly unbearable," I agreed, moving to untie you, now, rubbing your wrists and ankles. You stayed in the same position, your ass up. I said, "The others were drunk, too. They won't remember much. But you've known me forever, baby. The things you said...."

I positioned myself behind you, and I lifted the paddle again. "One to grow on," I said, "Remember?"

You nodded and held yourself firmly in place, no longer tied. I made the last one count, and you cried out at the sting. Then, composing yourself, you gingerly turned on your side and looked at me, rubbing your ass with one hand.

"It's been a long time since I was punished like that," you said, your eyes meek, humble.

"Too long," I said, waiting.

You moved, coming into my arms, hugging me. "I've missed being with you." Your hair was soft against my cheek. I felt my will sliding. I put my arms around you and stroked your back, then lifted your chin upward and kissed your lips.

"Me, too, baby," I said, softly. "Me, too."

Down and Dirty

Everyone has the potential. I'd like to start with that in my not-so-humble—and perhaps not-so-believable— defence. Everyone has the potential to surprise themselves in unforseen ways. You might think you're a good person. True to the core. You might live your life with that belief firmly implanted in your mind. And yet, if put in the right (or wrong) situation, you can fool even yourself.

Trust me. I know. Because that's what happened to me. I thought I was good. I thought I was one of those guys you could rely on. Honest and hard-working. A friend to the end.

And then I met you.

I wasn't supposed to like you. I mean, really like you. I could have liked you on the surface. Anyone would. I could have wanted to fuck you, to share a night of passion with you and then move on. Who wouldn't consider being with you? You're strikingly good looking, the type of good looking that makes people turn around for a double-take. But you weren't really my league. That's what my friends told me. You weren't someone in the business, someone who could understand the life I lead. No, you worked at a trendy bar nights and painted disturbing portraits during the days.

Even if I forgot about all that, I was taken—seriously taken.

Yet I fell. Fell hard and fast and down and dirty. Fell with you into the back of my car, fell onto the floor of your apartment. Fell so low that I couldn't see up anymore. And I have to say that I liked it. Fucking loved it. When you're clean—when you're well-behaved and polite all the time and say "please" and "thank you" in that careful way.... You don't know what dirty is.

But look who I'm talking to.

You know what dirty is. You know all about dirty.

Now, I do, too. And what I'm supposed to fucking do about it?

A silvery ringing fills my head and I close my eyes. The ringing stops abruptly and your husky voice replaces the bells. "Yeah?"

"Hey," I waver. "You busy?"

"No, baby, what's up?"

I hesitate, bringing my finger near the "disconnect" button, wondering, *"What am I doing? What in the hell am I doing?"*

"Nothing much," I lie. "Just wanted to talk to you."

"How're you and what's-her-name getting along?"

"Fine." I swallow. "Well, okay, I guess."

"Sounds great, baby," you respond, your voice filled with sarcasm. I hear the sound of a match as you light a cigarette. I imagine sitting across from you in your dark studio, watching you blow smoke rings toward the red-glossed ceiling. I imagine....

You inhale and ask, "If everything's fine, why are you calling me?"

Embarrassed silence on my end. My mind hissing, *"Everything's wrong. Everything's wrong. Everything...."*

"Never mind," you purr into the stone silence of my answer. Your voice is assuringly soft, but insistent. "What's on your mind?"

Your studio is in Hollywood, and the neon light from the club down below fills your apartment. When you lay naked on your floor, the red neon flickers over your body, illuminating your pale skin with a vibrant light. I like to stand across from you and watch you move. I like you to touch yourself while I watch. That's my favorite part. Practically, my favorite. The foreplay of watching you turn yourself on. Nothing comes close to that. Your fingers get slick as you slide them up and over your clit. You know exactly how to do it. Of course, you do. You know how to pinch your clit between your thumb and forefinger. How to just graze your clit with four of your fingers at once and then moan and arch your hips up off the painted concrete floor.

I watch as long as I can take before needing to replace your fingers with my mouth—my hungry, urgent mouth on you. On you there—

"Come on," you say. "Spill it—"

And that's just what I want to do. Spill everything. Stand over you, my hand working my cock at piston-speed as you continue to tug on your clit, until we both reach that point together. Jerking off side by side somehow has that dirty little edge that I need. The watching part.

"Talk to me," you insist, and I find my voice.

"We're steady," I say. "I mean, she thinks we are." Oh, fuck, I'm cruel and I know it. I've become the kind of guy that women's mothers warn them about. "But when we're in bed—"

"Fucking," you say.

"When we're in bed," I repeat, because she and I just don't fuck.

"You think about me?"

"It's the only way that I—"

"Can get excited." Not a question.

"Yeah."

"What do you need me to do? What do you dream about?"

I swallow hard, admitting something I'm ashamed to even think about. "We do it in the dark, with all the light's off. She brushes her teeth before... and after she hurries to the shower. She can't get in the shower fast enough. She's so damn clean." You'd have thought I'd said a bad word. *Clean.*

"And you need it rough and raw and dirty. You need the lights on to see the filth. You thought if you went with a nice girl it would rub off on you, didn't you?"

I nod. Can you believe it? That's what I thought. But it didn't work. And instead of getting cleaner, I am making my girlfriend dirty just by being with me. I am marking her with the deviousness of my thoughts, with the impurity of my desires.

"You want a bad girl again, don't you?" you ask, your voice crawling though my head, into my blood. Your voice beats in my heart. "You want everything that goes with it. The late nights. The club scene. The way it feels to go to sleep drenched in the scent of sex. Not bothering to shower right away. Or even right away in the morning. Reveling in that scent while you get your coffee. Standing in line at some cafe waiting for your espresso, and knowing that you just reek of sex."

I'm hard. Just from the way you talk, I'm hard. And from thinking about how we used to fit together. The dirty ways we used to play. I know why we split. I know all about it. But I think of you, going into a bar with me, making sure that by the end of the evening, I'd seen you kissing someone else. Or several someone elses. Making sure that I would be desperate to fuck you by the time we got home. Or before we got home. Up against the side of my truck. Or behind a restaurant, against a dumpster. Your body all I needed. *All* that I needed. Anywhere that we were.

Look, I thought it would be easier with someone else. Isn't that fucking cop-out? I thought my brain wouldn't be so fried, my body on fire all the fucking time. That I wouldn't be bothered about losing you. Worry about where you were or what you were doing.

"You want me," you say.

It makes me so damn hard when you talk to me. My own private 900 number. My own dirty fix. I want you to be on the floor, looking up at me. Your cold concrete floor. I want the canvases on the wall, half-finished. The ones that are faced to the wall that you're angry with right now. I want the overflowing ashtrays and the expensive bottle of vodka in the freezer. I want to know that there's probably nothing good for me in your fridge. Nothing healthy at all. But that I could open the door and find decadent foods that I would want to eat. Rich dark chocolates. Left-over Chinese from last night's food fest.

But really, I just want you. Watching me from the doorway, wearing only your low-cut jeans and a skimpy tank. Watching and knowing exactly what I need you to do. And then I want to take your place down there on the floor, and have you slide up against the wall and watch me. When I'm close to shooting, I want to feel the point of your stiletto heel on my shoulder, pushing me back down. I want the neon glare to blind me.

"If you're *really* good, I might just blow you. That's what you want, isn't it? That's what you need. If you behave yourself, I might suck you off. You know how much I like to swallow."

She doesn't like to do that. I can't even say the words 'oral sex' without her getting a pinched look on her face. But you. Man, your mouth—

"Right, baby?" you ask. "You remember."

I nod, but you can't see me. I roll over and stare at my reflection in the mirror on the back of our closet door. I see someone not all there, hazy, fading, slipping away.

"I want what we had," I find myself saying.

"Can't go back," you say, sounding darkly smug.

There's the sound of my new girlfriend's key in the lock. Opening the door, pulling me back to reality while driving me further away. I say, softly, "Look, I just have to see you," but the connection's dead and you're gone and she's walking down the hall toward our bedroom.

I hang up the phone. I look at the window.

I see the doorknob start to turn.

But I'm no longer there.

French Cut

You don't wear lingerie. It's not that you have anything against it, it's just not something you do. Your underwear is practical stuff: all-cotton Jockeys, sports bras, the occasional pair of boxers. I've never see lace gracing that beautiful, slim body of yours, never seen a Wonderbra caressing those firm breasts or a French-cut pair of panties on your pussy when we undress for the evening or to make love. You show a distrust of anything girlie, really, but clothing is where your sexy androgyny shows itself the most. You sleep in my old, threadbare tie-dye T-shirts, long enough to reach mid-thigh on your slight frame, and I'm not even sure you know the meaning of the word "stockings."

It all makes sense, really. You're a natural girl. No meat, just tofu, legumes, the rare slab of salmon. No drugs, just a few puffs off a joint when you're in the midst of your once-yearly party phase. No coffee, just herbal tea with a dollop of honey when you're feeling really naughty. No chocolate, just a sprinkling of carob chips mingling with nuts and berries in handfuls of savored trail mix. For you to wear lingerie would be as strange as a French whore downing a jug of Odwalla and a handful of chlorophyll and superfood tablets.

Which is why it grabs me when I see the lacy white thong riding up above the waist of your hiking shorts. I can't take my eyes off of it as I hurry to keep up with you on the difficult trail. For the first few minutes I want to tell you, want to sneak up behind you and whisper in your ear that I've noticed. But I remember your lecture, when we started hiking together, on wearing sensible underwear and cinching your belt tight enough that it doesn't slip down over your hips. I know there's a reason you've broken your own cardinal rules, and something tells me I'm going to find out.

We're close to the summit now, the isolated spot you've told me about where we can see the whole Golden Gate spread out below us like an impressionist tableau. I follow behind you with my cock tingling in my pants, hinting at a hard-on that wants so badly to come into being as my eyes linger on the French lace of your thong.

It happens, finally, when you stop and bend over to pick up a pine cone.

"Look," you say. "It's perfect." You've got a natural appreciation for pine cones — they're the seeds of the evergreen, though normally the reproductive potency of this one wouldn't have such an effect on me. Now, though, it causes my cock to grow hard in my shorts, quickly and painfully so that I have to shift and tug at my Jockeys.

Because, when you lean forward, I can see down your top — and see the hint of lace deep in your cleavage, the low-cut bra embracing your gorgeous breasts.

"Uncomfortable?" you ask, smiling, looking up at me, still bent over, cradling the phallic pine cone suggestively.

"Not at all," I say.

"Too bad," you tell me. You toss the pine cone off the trail and launch into a tawdry sprint, your hips swaying more than a hiking instructor would like.

Breathing hard already, I jog after you.

We reach the rocks sheened with sweat, your tank top so damp that when you slip off your backpack I can see the straps of the bra, tempting me even more. I follow you up the last bit of the trail, out onto the plateau of rocks and dirt sparsely covered with scrub.

"Isn't it gorgeous?" you ask, sweeping your hand over

the breathtaking view of the bridge, the ocean, and the bay. You bend over and start rummaging through your backpack; the thong climbs high, your hiking shorts falling further so I can see the curve of your ass.

"Gorgeous," I say.

You take out the blanket and spread it on the dry brown grass. You take out two plastic wine glasses, set the small cloth-insulated lunch box on the edge of the blanket and stretch beautifully in the slanted morning sunlight.

"It's awfully hot," you sigh. "Don't you think it's hot?"

"Sizzling," I say as I come toward you.

"Only one way to cool down," you tell me, and reach for the buckle of your belt.

I stop in my tracks, watching as you unfasten your belt and slide your shorts down your smooth, tanned legs. The skimpy thong you're wearing plunges so low I can see the top of your blonde hair, and there on the front of it, rimmed by lace, is a little pink heart.

You kick off your running shoes, slide off your socks, and reach down to pull up the sweat-soaked tank top. When you pull it over your head, I see that the bra matches the thong, a girlie push-up that makes your slight breasts look two cup sizes larger. The cups are so low-cut that they almost reach your nipples, which have gotten quite hard and are sticking plainly through the transparent sprinkling of lace. On the cups themselves is a pair of pink hearts, flawlessly matching the one on your pussy.

"I just love to undress out in nature," you smile as you see my eyes drinking in your lace-clad body. "Don't you?"

I take the hint, dropping my pack and stripping off my sweaty T-shirt, then kicking off my shoes and pulling down my hiking shorts and underwear as one. Your eyes linger over my erect cock, pointing toward you and slightly inclined like a come-hither finger begging you to come to me.

But I'm the one coming to you, I know. You lay down on the blanket, stretching deliciously out and turning from side to side so I can see both the infinitesimal string slid between your buttocks and the tiny patch of heart-adorned lace that covers your pussy. You smile flirtatiously.

"I went shopping yesterday while you were napping," you say. "I don't know what came over me."

I join you on the blanket, pressing my lips to yours and feeling your tongue surge into my mouth. My hand finds your nipples, feeling them harden still more under my touch, and the feel of them poking through the girlish lace excites me even more than I expect. Your fingers curve around my hard cock and you smile when our lips part.

"I'm hungry," you whisper. "Are you hungry?"

"Starving," I growl.

"Good," you tell me, and roll over, away from me. I reach out to touch your ass, fascinated by the unfamiliar way the lace thong looks against your tan.

You unzip the lunchbox and take out a small plastic baggie, frosted with condensation. You roll against me, pushing me onto my back and climbing atop me.

"Say 'aaaaaah,'" you tell me. "And close your eyes."

I do it, opening my mouth. The cold morsel I feel between my teeth shocks me; when I bite, I taste the mingling of forbidden dark chocolate with the taste of strawberries.

"Oh, wow," I mumble, my mouth full.

"Shhhhh," you say. "Just taste. Keep your eyes closed."

I savor the taste of it, ripe and invigorating. I hear you chewing, and when you kiss me, your lips taste of chocolate and strawberry. "Keep your eyes closed!" you laugh.

I feel you reaching out to the lunch box. You place a chilled orb in my mouth and when I bite down I feel the sugared juice of a cherry overwhelming me. You kiss me, hard, your tongue slipping in and lapping at the syrupy confection.

"One last time," you say. "Sit up a little. Keep your eyes closed."

I hear the twist of a screw-top, the faint glug of liquid. You place the rim of the plastic glass in my mouth, and your hand on the back of my head, telling me when to tip. Red wine floods my mouth, and I feel it dribble warm onto my chest even as I recognize the aromatic flavor — Merlot.

"Messy, messy," you say, bending down to lick the droplets of wine off my chest. Your tongue remains against my skin as you lick up to my throat, then kiss me, your mouth tasting of sweet chocolate, fruit and wine. You take a drink yourself and curl up on top of me, the soft lace of your bra caressing my face as it darkens from the droplets of red wine still slicking my lips.

"I would have brought a cigar," you tell me. "But that would have been going too far."

I'm overwhelmed; I have to have you. My mouth finds your nipple through the lace and I bite gently, suckling it into my mouth. You gasp softly as my tongue deftly pushes the lace down so I can get to the smoothness of your erect bud. Then you're moaning, as my hands cup your ass and gently tug the lacy crotch of your thong out of the way.

"If I'd known chocolate and wine would have this kind of effect on you," you sigh as I guide you onto my cock, "I would have done this months ago."

Then you're not speaking, you're moaning, as I feel the head of my cock parting your lips, feel you sliding down onto me, hungry with need, my shaft filling your cunt as my mouth teases your nipple. The lace against my cheeks feels strange, erotic — but that's not the reason I want you, nor is it the chocolate or the wine that's intoxicated me. It's the feel of your cunt around my shaft, the desperation with which you slide my cock deep into you.

When I grasp your buttocks and roll you over onto your

back, the wine goes flying and spreads a dark stain across the blanket. Neither of us pauses, even as the bottle tips and a stream of Merlot begins to pool under you. I slide into you deeper, your legs going easily up onto my shoulders as I pick up the bottle and empty it over your breasts.

"My new bra," you breathe, only able to mock despair for the faintest instant before my cock reaches its deepest point inside you and you thrust up against me, your lips open wide. I lick red wine from your breasts as you clutch me tight, your hands running through my hair, your body meeting mine with each hungry thrust. By the time you're ready to come, I've reached out and snatched another chocolate from the baggie.

"Open your mouth and say 'aah,'" I tell you, and my thumb teases open your lips just far enough to slip the treasured chocolate cream onto your tongue. You take the whole thing in one bite, your eyes closed, savoring the sensations. I'll never know if you actually come at the very moment you taste the chocolate, because you're one of those girls who comes so hard and so long that isolating your moment of pleasure is next to impossible. But the twist of your body and the arch of your back tells me that it's close enough for lovers. I fuck you harder as you chew the cream and swallow, your moan rich and thick around the textured confection.

Then I shut my eyes tight, on the very brink of orgasm, and I should expect it — but I don't.

Somehow, without missing a beat, without lessening your own pleasure, you've managed to reach out and snatch a lemon creme from the baggie, even as it opens and the chocolates scatter across your belly. Your fingers pop the creme into my mouth and its taste fills me at the instant I come, orgasm and sweetness blending in an instant as I thrust deep into you, feeling myself clench far inside your body.

When I feel your legs descending from my shoulders, your thighs caressing my sides, I settle on top of you and feel the squish of chocolates between us, coating your skin and mine in the melted ooze of indulgence.

My tongue licks the chocolate from your breasts, feeling only a small tinge of sadness as I look at your ruined bra. You unhook it and squirm out of the bra, then reach down and slide off the thong, looking distastefully at it as I see that the chocolates and wine have run down, staining the pink heart with our jealously-guarded vices.

You toss the lingerie into the brush, leaving them for some lucky hiker to puzzle over. You smile up at me, your face and breasts moist with wine and melted chocolate, looking, somehow, even more lascivious than the skimpy lace did.

"See?" you sigh. "I never should have let that lingerie salesgirl talk me into this. What have I been telling you? Chocolate and wine are filthy habits." You snuggle up closer to me, our skin sliding together with the mixture of drink and debauchery.

And when I kiss you, I taste them both. Sweet, like you, and just as forbidden.

Handyman

I know exactly what you're going to do from the first day we come to your house to do the work. Maybe I know it even before you do, yourself. Before you realize how this passion play is going to unfold. See, it's simple. I know from the start that you're going to choose one of the three of us. Just one. Isn't it lucky for you to have such a selection? I've already summed up your choices in my head: of our trio— one's too young. Another too much into the job to notice you, even with your gray-green eyes and your full, kissable mouth. Even with the way you move your body, the slinky style you have of walking, that special way you stride even in high heels. But the third is me. *I'm* the one who watches everywhere you go—the one who winks and gives a low chuckle when you try to talk about building with us. You might know a lot about a broad variety of subjects, from ancient artifacts to political pundits, but you're pitifully lacking when it comes to engaging in small-talk about construction work.

Yet that doesn't bother me at all. Because at the end of the day, I'm the one who's destined to pick you up, strip you down, spread you out on a wooden horse. Man, do you look amazing, but I can't stop to admire you yet. First, it's time to use my belt to fasten your wrists together. And then it's time to fuck you—not with my cock at the beginning, but with my screwdriver. The handle smooth and rounded inside you, the metal part cool in my hand.

See? I know all about you. I've watched you look at me when I work. And not just at me, but at my toolbox. I have gauged your interest, and I notice the way you start to stutter, to stumble over words when I reach for different items in my heavy metal tool kit.

I like the way you look at my tools. The heat in your cheeks as I fondle different implements. You want to feel the heavy weight inside you. You want me to fuck you, or fix you, with each of the colorful plastic handles. More sexy than sex toys. Far more sexy. Because these are utilitarian items. They aren't fake contraptions, or molded plastic dildos meant to look like a man's cock. These are real. That's the difference. That's why you like them.

I'm right. When you ask me to stay after work, when you ask me to help you fix something else, just one more thing that slipped your mind, I know I'm right. I carry my box with me to your bedroom, and I'm sure that you don't have a squeaky hinge here or a window that can't be unstuck. I watch knowing exactly what's going to happen as if I've seen this movie before. But I haven't. It's all new to me as you strip down and spread your legs and you beg me with your eyes to do what I have to do.

Quickly, I reach for my favorite tool. The lovely screwdriver that is the king of my toolbox. Yeah, it's lovely. I can say that, can't I? It's so well-crafted, so smooth and sleek. I do what I fantasized about from the moment I saw you. I part your pussy lips with my slightly calloused fingers and I slide the tool inside you, the handle of it disappearing within your slippery pussy.

Oh, god, baby. The way your eyes change. They go flat—matte—unflinching as I work that tool inside of your body. You contract on it. I can tell. You want more. I rock it back and forth, and you groan. I slide it almost all the way out of you, and you beg me to keep fucking you with it.

I can do that. I can give you everything you need. My fingertips are all wet with your juices as I keep plunging the tool inside of you. You lift your hips up off the bed, meeting me, helping me. I can only imagine how good this must feel. The cool molded plastic thick and smooth inside you. I've never seen a woman so wet before. How long have you fantasized about this? I don't ask. Probably as long as I've fantasized about this, too. Right?

Then you gaze right into my eyes, and I see that now, you want more. Now, you want me.

That's fine. I'm ready for you. I can fix anything you want. Anything you need.

Five Senses

I hear the door creak open. Then I hear footsteps, a mix of bare feet and, I suppose, high-heeled shoes on the carpet of our living room. I keep my hands pressed firmly on either side of me, the velveteen couch soft against them. I take a deep breath and smell a mingled bouquet of perfumes and female bodies. I look into the darkness and listen for the next cue.

The first thing I feel are lips, against mine, kissing me. One tender, soft kiss, its taste familiar, the brush of your smooth cheek against mine, your fingertips tracing a path down my chest to the top of my boxer shorts. Then you're gone, and I feel another kiss, someone else's, the unfamiliar taste of a new woman, her tongue grazing my lips very gently. Her hand caresses my cheek, then my neck. Then there's another kiss, from someone new, someone more aggressive with her tongue, forcing it deep into my mouth, kissing me hungrily, her teeth nipping my lower lip. Then two more kisses in rapid succession, one on my lips while someone else licks my ear with the tip of her tongue. I don't know whether to count four or five, and I suppose it doesn't matter, because I'll never know.

The music starts, slow and sensual, a chilled trance with a dark, erotic feel. I sense a body near me; then I feel her thighs on either side of mine as she climbs onto me.

Her breasts, naked, brush my face, their firm nipples teasing my lips gently apart. She dances in time with the music, her fingers stroking my face as she grinds on top of me. Slowly, she lowers herself into my lap and I feel the press of her pussy, through my boxer shorts and what feels like a G-string, against my crotch. My cock stretches hard against the shorts.

The music grows louder, rising in intensity. The woman atop me dances more vigorously, her body rocking back and forth as she presses her crotch to mine. I hear whispering, distantly, mixed in with the music, and a faint spray of giggles. There are five of you, total, I'm sure of it.

Then I feel someone leaning over the back of the couch, feel a kiss on the side of my neck. I take a deep breath and smell you just as the woman dancing for me leans forward, and I hear—or perhaps sense—the two of you kissing.

She reaches down and touches my cock, gently stroking it through the thin, damp fabric of my boxer shorts. Her fingers close tight around it, gently kneading my shaft.

Then again—maybe they're your fingers. That's the beautiful, terrifying part. I'll never, ever know.

"Lap dancing is sexy," I told you. "There's something really erotic about not being able to touch."

"But you can still see everything," you said.

"Yes, you can…see, smell, feel with the rest of your body. You can hear her breathing, hear her talking to you. You can even taste her."

"Taste her?"

"Well," I said. "Sometimes they kiss."

"Not in clubs," you told me. "Do they kiss you in clubs?"

"Not usually," I said. "But sometimes, if they're breaking the rules. And they want a big tip."

"Is that hot?"

"Incredibly."

"And if you weren't in a club — say, if a woman was dancing for you at home?"

"With the same rules?"

"Well," you smirked. "I think if it was at home you'd be allowed to taste a little more. But not touch."

I smiled. "Yes," I said. "I think that would be hot."

"Would it be hot even if you couldn't see? If you were, say, blindfolded?"

"Yes," I said. "I think that would be incredibly hot."

"Because then you'd have to use all of your five senses?"

I laughed. "Four," I said. "I'd only have four senses."

And you smiled at me, looking mischievous, exceptionally naughty.

"No, you'd have five. Because you could imagine how good she looked on top of you."

"Yes," I said. "I guess I could."

"I know you love to let your imagination run wild," you said, caressing my face. "I think that would be the ultimate thing for you. Being lap-danced by more than one woman, say, never knowing which was touching you at any one time. Maybe never even knowing who they were, what they looked like."

I looked at you suspiciously. "Why?" I asked you.

"Well," you smiled coquettishly. "You do have a birthday coming up…"

She turns around in my lap, spreading her legs and sitting down on my cock. I can feel the strap of her G-string against the shaft of my cock. She grinds her smooth, full buttocks against me, wiggling her ass back and forth in time with the music.

The way she's stroking me with her ass feels more incredible than I could have dreamed. She leans back against me, her back naked against my bare chest, her shoulders rubbing my face. Her skin drapes over me, curtaining my face in the scent of her. She reaches back and caresses my face. I hear her breathing heavily as she rocks against me, her soft sighs rising in time with the music.

I hear whispers, giggles. Apparently this first dancer is hogging all the fun.

She lifts herself off of me, and I feel another body against mine. Her breasts brush my face again. This one is wearing a lace top, her breasts fuller and heavier than the other. The lace feels rough against my lips, especially with her nipples stretching it so taut. She smells different, floral, more perfumed. I feel the press of heavier fabric against my cock, hear the creak of leather; she's wearing a leather G-string, possibly, or maybe leather hot pants.

She lifts up her lace top and brushes her naked tits over my face. I breathe deeply of her scent, let my lips part slightly, let my tongue laze out to taste her flesh. She's salty but somehow sweet. She pushes her nipple between my lips and I suckle it gently as she grinds her crotch down onto mine. I'm moaning softly, the sound muffled by her nipple. As she bends forward I don't feel her hair at first; as she rubs the top of her head over my face, I feel that she's got short hair, cropped in what must be a cute little pixie-cut. Is it your friend Shauna, I wonder, or is it some dancer you've hired for the evening? Would a dancer let me suckle her breasts like this? Would Shauna? Then I feel the hot pants grinding hard against me, her pussy deep inside them, and I remember how sexy Shauna looked in her little leather outfit that one time we all got dolled up for dancing. She squirms on top of me and I feel her upper body, bare against mine as she rubs the lace shirt over my face. I inhale deeply of her scent. She slips the lace away and discards it. Her lips press against mine and I feel her tongue working its way into my mouth; in that instant, I let it go, not caring whether it's Shauna or a complete stranger, a college girl making $200 an hour. I only care that her tongue is warm, slick, soft in my mouth. And that her breasts, now naked, are gently brushing my chest, her nipples hard and inviting so that when she slides up my body and moves them into my mouth, they feel better against my tongue than anything I could have wanted.

When she eases herself off of me, I feel the caress of gentle fingers down my front, sliding into my boxer shorts and wrapping around my cock, stroking it. That must be you, mustn't it? You would never let another woman, friend or stripper, touch my cock directly — would you? But when I feel lips against mine, taste the salt of a woman's tongue, I know it's not you — the way she kisses is different, entirely, than the way you do it. As she strokes my cock she dances in time with the music, rubbing against me. She's wearing nothing but a crop-top she's pulled up over her breasts, and when she slips her hand out of my shorts and sits in my crotch, legs spread, I can feel the moistness of her naked pussy rubbing up and down against my cock through my boxer shorts. I hear myself moaning uncontrollably; the touch of a naked pussy, even through the cotton of my shorts, feels so good I'm afraid I'm going to come. She sits down hard in my crotch, firmly wiggling her ass back and forth as she leans back and reaches to caress my face, her long hair sweeping across my shoulders. It's so long I can feel it down my chest, almost reaching her ass. Monique, I wonder? Your friend from the office, who you once made out with at a bar after work? I inhale deeply, smelling the faint hint of hibiscus shampoo, the barest suggestion of sharp, musky feminine sweat. She moves in time with the music and I want to reach down, slip my cock out of my shorts, and slide into her. Except that those aren't the rules, and I would never break them — because then this torment would end, and it's the most delicious torment I've ever known, a torment for all my five senses.

Monique—or whoever— rises off of me and I feel another woman climbing into my lap, this one smaller, with very slight breasts she uses to tease my lips. Her nipples are very large and extremely hard, and it excites me to taste the new taste, so very slightly different than the last woman. I imagine her, cataloging your address book of adventurous friends — and knowing, all the while, that I probably don't know her. Is she beautiful, I wonder? It doesn't matter, because the touch of her nipples on my mouth is electric, sending a surge to my cock, and I'm quite clear that however beautiful she is, I'll never know it. I suckle on her nipples gently as she settles down on me, rubbing her crotch against mine. She's wearing shorts, possibly spandex, but they're so skintight that I can feel the lips of her pussy against my cock, even through the boxer shorts. I smell her and detect the aroma of sandalwood, lost in a mix of feminine lust and the sharp scent of pussy. She swings around and sits in my lap, facing out, her ass slim and slight against my cock. She reaches back and parts her cheeks gently so she can slide my cock between them, the head popping free of my boxers to stroke her through the spandex. When she leans back, grinding in time with the music, I feel her hair, curly and long, caressing my face. It smells faintly of the smoke of clove cigarettes, sweet and exotic, and when she rises off of me, I miss it.

Then there's another body on mine, unfamiliar. I smell sex, hard and sharp in the sweat-heated room. The woman kisses me, hard, her tongue plunging inside me, her ample breasts tight against my chest, nipples hard. She grinds her crotch against mine, and she's so wet that I feel the front of my boxers soaking through. She's naked — fully naked, not guarded by any of the scraps of fabric that each of my previous tormenters wore. She kisses me harder than you do, more insistent, more unforgiving. She tastes so salty it's almost like blood, and she smells so sharply of sex any other perfume would be lost. When she reaches into my boxers and wraps her hand around my cock, she grips it hard enough to almost make me come.

But she knows men's bodies well enough to keep me from climaxing, and she deftly slips my cock out through the fly of my boxers. What she does then shocks me.

I feel her pussy enveloping the head of my cock. Surely she's teasing, isn't she? You would never let another woman fuck me. Or would you?

Then she sits down, forcing my cock deep inside her.

She moans so loud I recognize the voice immediately. She grinds her hips on top of me, pushing my cock up hard against the depths of her cunt. She wraps her arms around me and pulls me closer, her lips finding mine and her tongue delving deep into my mouth. She starts fucking me with a fury, a desperation, a passion you've never shown. She's fucking me for *her* pleasure, and if I come inside her it's only incidental. Her sighs and moans mount quickly toward a peak.

I think I'm going to hold back, to let her come first. But I don't, because she comes so fast it surprises me when she grabs me and clenches me tight against her. Her body goes rigid for an instant, her hips immobilized in the explosion of pleasure. Then she's fucking me again, her body sliding up and down the shaft of my cock, juice dribbling out and soaking my boxers. It's only an instant more before I come, my ass lifting off the sofa, my mouth open in a cry of ecstasy.

She kisses my face all over, familiar kisses as I breathe a familiar smell. Why I didn't recognize it at first, I don't know — except that the five of you — or four, or six, or seven — had awakened my five senses so much that I smelled new things in the familiar aroma of your pussy.

When you rise off of me, I feel my cock slick with my come and your pussy. You sigh, whisper to me to keep the blindfold on. I hear whispers, giggling voices. Familiar, unfamiliar — who knows? With so many senses, I'm bewitched and misled at every opportunity.

I hear footsteps as you all leave the room. It's only when I've heard the door close that I take a deep breath and pull off the blindfold. I squint into the light.

The dancers' clothes, all of them, shoes included, rest discarded in a pile on the coffee table. When they walked out of this room, they were all naked — leaving me to wonder. Did I really recognize the sound of your moans, the feel of your pussy, the explosion of your orgasm? Or was it another woman who made love to me, as you watched, as you directed her, enjoying the sight of me lost in the oblivion of five senses?

That's the beautiful part, you see.

Because I'll never, ever know.

Body Shots

You're wearing a robe when you answer the door—a robe, and not much else. Maybe nothing—it seems quite possible that you're nude underneath that sexy robe, and you're certainly not far from it. It's not much of a robe, either, to tell you the truth. I don't recognize the flimsy garment; when we were together, you tended toward terrycloth, sweats and T-shirts.

It's a little white satin thing, frosted with lace around the neckline and clingy—though not quite see-through. I can see the swell of your breasts underneath it, and you're not wearing shoes.

"Hi," you say, seeming a little less surprised than I expect you to be.

"I'm sorry," I answer. "I didn't mean to wake you up."

"I wasn't asleep yet," you tell me. "I was reading. What's up?" You're looking at me with a guarded expression of distaste, and I realize that I've made a mistake.

"I...I was in the neighborhood," I lie. "I thought I'd drop by and see if you wanted to get a drink. You've already gotten in bed. I'll go."

You shrug. "No, don't be silly. I wasn't going to bed yet. Come in."

"You want to get a drink?"

You look at me distrustfully, and I swear I see your eyes flicker over me, as if you're trying to remember what my body looks like under the clothes. "I don't feel like getting dressed."

"No problem," I say. "I'll go."

You smile. "No. Come in."

I walk into your apartment and its smell hits me like a vivid memory. There's a special smell each person has, and when it's as familiar as yours is to me, it's sometimes a little scary how much it can evoke. Yours is the scent of houseplants—ferns, flowers and cactus—mingled with the smell of lavender—bath products, body oil, and hand soap. Lingering underneath it all is the scent of that sexy perfume you sometimes wear when you're going out—and I'm a little surprised when I realize that the last scent is a little stronger than it ought to be.

My suspicion is confirmed when I see your little black dress discarded in the middle of the living room, mixed in with a tangle of garter belt, thong panties, and bra, with the twin mounds of balled-up fishnet stockings hovering on either side. I caught you coming home early from a club, perhaps—after all, it is midnight.

"I didn't think I'd catch you at home," I say, breathing deeply and juggling the knowledge of your scents in my memory.

"Well, you did," you say. "I've got Corona, Bud and Blackened Voodoo Lager."

"Voodoo," I say.

You stand there looking incredible in that tiny robe, the curves of your body barely hidden by its thin, satiny fabric.

"It's a year old," you tell me.

"All right, then. Corona."

"It's *two* years old."

"Ummmm…."

"I should know better than to offer you Bud."

"It'll do," I say.

"Of course," you sigh, your lips twisted in a frown. "You know me. I've also got tequila."

"You got limes?"

You roll your eyes. "Puh-leeze."

"All right," I smile. "Sounds great."

I sit on the little loveseat, the only place there is to sit in your small living room. I savor the smell of you, feeling it hit me that underneath all the lavender, ferns and perfume there's that unmistakable essence I came to love so much but never put a name on—because it's got your name, the scent of your body, the scent of your lust. Or maybe it's the scent of *my* lust, because smelling it makes me want you even more than I already do. I wonder briefly if you still taste the same.

You come out holding a bottle of Cuervo, a Bud, a handful of limes and a knife. Tucked into the belt of your little white robe is a canister of Morton's table salt. The weight of it has tugged your belt open just a bit, and your robe is falling away from the slope of your breasts, revealing them almost to the point that I can see your nipples. I try hard not to look, but it's hopeless. I can't keep my gaze away from you. My eyes rove over your tits, remembering how good they feel against my body, against my face.

"I don't have any shot glasses," you say. "Hope you don't mind swapping spit."

"Not at all," I tell you.

You cut a lime into quarters, pour some salt on your hand. You hold out your hand. I look at you, puzzled, until you nod at the little pile of salt. I lean forward and lick it, the taste of the salt mingling with your familiar smell. You hand me the bottle of tequila and I take a swig. As I swallow, you push a lime wedge into my mouth and I suck. I remember this taste from a long time ago; I haven't drunk tequila since the last time I smelled you close up. You smile.

"Body shots, remember?"

"I always thought 'body shots' sounded like it should be something more lascivious," I say.

You beam. "Well it can be," you say. "If you want it to. You should remember that part, too. I mean, it hasn't been *that* long."

I nod, sucking at the lime.

You pour salt onto your hand again, lick it, down the tequila from the bottle and slip a wedge in your mouth.

"So what do you want to talk about?" you mumble around the lime wedge.

I take mine out of my mouth and reach out for the tequila. I take a long pull of it, straight, still tasting the lime and salt. I pour salt on my hand and hold it out for you.

You take the lime slice out of your mouth just long enough to lick my hand and gulp some tequila; then you shove it back in and smile at me wickedly.

"You're trying to get me drunk," you say, your voice muffled by citrus.

I look at the way the white, lacy satin robe is falling open in front, now open almost to your belly button, showing me the sides of your full breasts and the smoothness of your upper stomach. You look incredible, if a little strange with lime rind filling your mouth.

"What gave you that idea?"

"Who comes over to his ex-girlfriend's house at midnight to drink tequila, anyway? This is a booty call."

"Is that right?" I sprinkle salt directly on my tongue, take another drink, suck lime. "If I recall, you suggested the tequila," I mumble in lime dialect.

"Guilty," you say. "You seeing anyone?"

I'm feeling slightly drunk now. My eyes linger over your breasts. "I'm definitely seeing something I like, at the moment."

You glance down, look up at me, and smile. You take the lime wedge out of your mouth and conspicuously fail to pull your robe shut.

"See? Booty call."

I'm already hard, your smell, the tequila and the sight of your gorgeous body barely clad in white lace making me anything but my usual reserved self. I lean forward and slip my hands into your robe, closing my palms over your breasts.

Your nipples are hard, and it's not at all cold in here.

As the robe comes open, I see that you're nude underneath it. Your naked body looks gorgeous, familiar, exciting. I want it so bad it hurts. I kiss you, tasting you even over the salt and citrus and agave. Our tongues meet and you lean forward into me as my hands caress your tits. You're breathing hard, scared or turned on or both. My thumbs press your nipples and you moan softly, wriggling deeper into my grasp. I bend forward and lick each nipple, feeling you shiver with each stroke of my tongue.

"Want more tequila?" you ask, nervously.

"Sure," I say, reaching out and snatching the salt. I push you down onto the couch, your eyes going wide as you giggle drunkenly.

I delicately salt your nipples, grab the tequila, and lick.

You giggle when I lick one nipple, almost upsetting the small pile of salt I've built on the other one. Salt scatters over your belly as I take a swig of tequila.

"Oh, see? Now I've got my work cut out for me."

I lick up and down your belly, tasting the salt of your sweat mixed with Morton's. You breathe harder, writhing under the stroke of my tongue. When I close my mouth over your salty nipple, your arms come around my head, pulling me close, and I bite lightly, lapping up the salt.

When I lift my head, I gulp tequila and stick a lime in my mouth. I smile around it, daring you.

"Two can play at that game," you say. "Get undressed."

It's been a long time since I heard you say that, but I'm not going to question your motives—or either of our drunkenness. We haven't had *that* much tequila. I stand up and quickly strip off my clothes, leaving a pile at the edge of the sofa. Your eyes rove over my hard cock, and you smile.

"You do still love me," you giggle.

I lay back down and you lean over me. You squeeze cold lime juice over my hard cock and I gasp.

"Let's just do it all in one kiss, shall we?" You sprinkle salt over my cock and your mouth finds me, hard, sucking me into your mouth. You don't stop with a lick, though; your lips slide up and down my shaft, bringing moans from behind the lime. You give me just enough to tease me mercilessly; then you sit up and swig from the bottle.

"Too salty," you smile. "Needs more lime." You stuff a lime wedge in your mouth as I reach for the salt.

Spitting the lime indelicately across your apartment, I push you onto your back again and spread your legs. You don't resist, don't hesitate; you let me guide your thighs wide open as I get on my knees and sprinkle salt over your pussy.

"Hope you haven't shaved recently," I tell you, and descend on your pussy like a starving man. The salt taste overwhelms me for a moment, but then it's lost in the lush tang of your pussy and the surge I feel in my cock as I start to eat you out. It tastes so familiar yet faraway, and it makes me want more. My tongue wriggles into your entrance and I taste you, wet, salty, better than Cuervo Gold. I press my tongue on your clit and listen to you moan through the thick wedge of lime.

"Drink," you say. "You're spoiling the body shot."

My mouth comes away from your pussy, just an inch. "I'm done with tequila," I say. "I'm on the wagon."

Then my mouth returns to your pussy, pressing hard against it, licking you hungrily as your hips rock against my face. Your hands rest on my shoulders and I hear you whispering my name, then moaning it, then gasping, groaning it, and I don't even think to wonder when you lost the lime. I eat you out forever, listening to you mount toward orgasm, knowing from years of experience how to back off at just the right instant to keep you hovering on the brink.

"Fuck," you whimper. "Please, let me come? I'll give you all the body shots you can handle, just please, make me come."

My fingers slide easily into you, finding your G-spot and massaging firmly. You're begging for it, now, shameless in your desire for me. You push me onto the floor and climb on top of me, your thighs wrestling my head to the floor as you force your pussy desperately onto my mouth again. And then your mouth is on my cock—no salt needed.

My hands cup your buttocks as I work your clit, the tip of my tongue as alive with sensation as the shaft of my cock as you suck me. Moaning, you pump your hips, working your pussy against my face. My cock glides into your mouth, down your throat, your hands caressing my balls as you propel yourself toward orgasm on my eagerly seeking tongue. When you climax, you grip my cock and breathe hot and hard on it, my tongue riding your clit until the strength goes out of your body and you relax on top of me, too exhausted from your pleasure to do anything but gently kiss my cock, your tongue lazing up and down the shaft.

I lift you up, set you on the couch. Taking your hand, I glance toward the bedroom.

"Sure," you say. "Why not? It's just a different kind of body shot, right?"

We don't even make it to the bed. We hit the carpeted floor hard, so hard I'm afraid I've hurt one of us. But if you care, you don't let me know. You just spread your legs and pull me into you, your pussy so wet my cock fills it in a single thrust. We claw toward the bed half-heartedly for a moment, then lose ourselves in the thrust of me fucking you, the arch of your back as you come for the second time, the moan from my lips as I come inside you, clutching you close, holding you.

I feel your kisses on the side of my face, listen to your breathing gradually slowing to normal. My cock slips out of you, and I realize your pristine white robe is stained with liquor, sweat and come.

"Whew," you sigh. "How I love what tequila does for me."

It was rare, in the old days, for us to make love twice in a row. But the second we crawl into bed together, I know it's going to happen. This time I eat you out luxuriously for long, slow minutes, feeling your body surge against mine, loving every minute because I know there's little chance you'll come again. But when I enter you, from behind this time so I can touch those gorgeous breasts I've missed so much, so that I can kiss you on the back of the neck while I fuck you, the way you like, you come almost immediately, not even touching your clit. And I know, even in the swirling fog of your bedroom, it isn't the tequila.

"Were you really in the neighborhood?" you ask me, when the sun breaks through the window of your bedroom.

I think about it for a minute.

"Sure," I say. "Absolutely."

You look at me suspiciously.

"Then perhaps you could arrange to be 'in the neighborhood' next weekend, too?"

I nod, smiling softly.

You wriggle closer to me, your face tucked against my neck.

"Good," you tell me. "I've been needing a new drinking partner."

"I told you," I smile. "I'm on the wagon."

You giggle, sounding still a little drunk, though I know you must be long sober by now.

"What a shame," you tell me. "I guess we'll have to find something else to do."

The Beginning

Start at the beginning.

Start with the strident howl of the alarm bringing me into slow-spreading hazy consciousness this morning, your warm body curled spoon-like in my arms. I don't want to move you to hit the 'off' switch. You feel so right there, so perfect. Your body is cradled against me, your shiny red hair spread in tiny corkscrew curls over my neck and chest—a fire-haired angel, all warm and soft and breathing in the rhythm of your dreams, unpunctured by my alarm.

Carefully, I untangle one arm and turned off the noise. Then I move away from you so that I won't disturb your sleep. I want to think. I want to figure this all out. Yet I can't take my eyes off you. Never has a woman so captivated me while doing nothing. Nothing but sleeping, that is.

You look like a model in a pre-Raphaelite painting I saw in Italy a few summers ago, the nymph floating downstream with her eyes closed and hands folded over her breasts, a halo hovering inches above her head.

After a moment, I settle back against the down-filled pillows and try to recreate the events of the previous evening. But last night was not the real beginning. No, not by far. And yet, the beginning isn't so clear to me. Only the summery smell of your tan body when we moved together from the doorway to the bed, the feel of your white slip with the tiny straps, so light and dainty beneath my fingertips. I caressed the silky material, caressed the satin of your skin, as we fell together on my nest of a bed. *That* wasn't the beginning by far—it was the culmination. The peak.

How you felt beneath me was unreal—god, so warm and open. I pushed your slip away, up past your hips, and found that you'd already taken your panties off while I was undressing. Sliding my hands up to your pussy, I felt just how wet you were. Wet and ready.

I'd wanted to be there for such a long time, at the split of your legs, my mouth right up against you, tongue twirling in circles up and over your clit. You moaned and lifted your hips, helping me, and when you said my name, I thought I'd come on the mattress. Sure, you've said my name a lot of times before. But never like that. Never like a drawn-out sigh, all rich with pleasure.

With you asleep now, I recall each frame of last night's living movie. But that's not what I want to think about. All that's doing is just making me hard. What I want to figure out is how you knew, how you set us up to reach this place. So now, I try harder, picturing the two of us in a similar embrace on the dance floor, moving in sexy circles in the center of the club, directly under the mirrored disco ball. Beneath those shimmering rainbows of light, it was evident what would happen, it was certain what the future held.

But even *that* wasn't the beginning.

Maybe the real start of the story is the day I first saw you, the moment we were first introduced.

"Over here," my boss called, motioning me to his side in the lunchroom. "This is our new art director," he said, pointing to you. "Just taking her on a tour." He continued to describe how this was your first day, and how you seemed to be getting on well with the staff, how you could 'hold your own.' I'll admit I hardly could speak when it was my turn. I was in a complete daze as I heard him discuss my job title, "chief story editor." It was almost as if he were speaking another language. I saw you and I wanted you. We shook hands, checking each other out.

Friend or foe? Ally or enemy?

I remember holding your hand a few beats too long, a few moments past the designated hand-shake time, that internal clock that everyone seems to own. I remember your face as you sized me up, then smiled, the corners of your crimson-glossed mouth turning up at the edges. I thought, "Red lipstick on a redhead." I've dated girls with hair your color before, and I've hard them talk. Red's no good for redheads, right? So how do you get away with that? I don't know how, but you manage to break all the stated rules, don't you? You always know what looks good. I guess it goes along with being an art director—or maybe being an art director goes along with understanding style.

We were instant friends, which is a rarity among co-workers, I know, and even harder to explain since we crossed the male/female sex barrier. Yet something about our senses of humor, our outlooks on life just plain clicked. Out to lunch to sit on the front steps of our office building and eat pretzels from the stand. Out in the evening to hit the bars near your apartment in West Hollywood or mine in Venice. I know that people talked from the beginning. How many girls and guys pal around together? At least, ones who aren't fucking? But it wasn't like that. Weekends we spent at movies or barbecuing or out at Dodger games.

Always there was something there. I mean that always there was a *beginning* of something. The spark before the catch of a flame, the trickle-splatter of raindrops on the sidewalk before the storm hits. So finding a starting place is hard for me now—with your smooth warm body nestled against mine. It just seems as if it has always been this way.

Of course, there *was* a moment when we went from friends to lovers. Literally, hands-on, flesh-to-flesh, and that moment happened last night. But I will be vague again and say that I craved you from that over-long beat of your fingertips against mine. Yearned for you when those darkly painted lips turned upwards in a grin of satisfaction.

I've wanted you from the start.

Yesterday evening, we went to Lula's, our favorite bar, down the street from our Brentwood office. We had a few drinks each, frozen Margaritas and shots of honey-hued tequila. Then, apparently feeling bold with the power of the booze, you mentioned a new club in your part of town that you'd read about. I was game, ready for a change from our usual digs, and we hopped into my silver Alfa, put the top down, and sped along Wilshire toward Santa Monica Blvd.

We parked without a problem, just down the street from Tower Records, then walked into the club. I looked at you in the semi-darkness. The disco lights, multi-colored spirals, flickered over your face, making your golden wolf-eyes go flat and yellow and matte.

"C'mon," you urged, pulling gently toward the bar, and I followed, moving slowly but somehow right to the beat of the dance music, the singer's voice sending ripples of harmony into the atmosphere. The beat of the song become one with the pounding roar of my blood in my ears.

At the bar with our fresh drinks, I felt your hand on my thigh, just resting there, and when a toughlooking punk asked you to dance, you shook your head "no." You were with me. I have to say, I felt elated, as if I'd been the first kid on the playground chosen for the kickball team. Then I felt something else, a tightness in my throat, a hardness between my legs....*Be honest*, I admonished myself. *Wasn't that demanding hardness there whenever you and I were together?*

I didn't have time to answer the nagging inner voice. You took the frosted glass from my hand and leaned in close to me to whisper, "Will you dance with me?" a pause, then, "Please?" the desire in your voice undeniable. Would I ever deny that lilting voice anything? Any request at all?

Your full breasts brushed my arm slightly; your fingers played up and down the sleeve of my gray shirt. Then your fingertips pressed against my wrist, as if feeling my pulse, as if reading me, and that simple touch opened a new world for me. The base feel of your fingers on my veins, reading my life lines, the rivers of my blood, suddenly made everything clear. There was power in your touch, power that I had felt on our very first meeting. But now the shift of it, from you to me to you again, was tangible, and I was standing before my brain was even aware of my body's actions.

I took your hand and we walked together to the dance floor. I caught the approving stares right away, the stares of men who looked longingly at you. I followed the route of their gazes, catching the way your slender hips shimmied to the beat, your mane, a ring of fire, changing beneath the vibrant lights.

Red. Gold. Copper.

Your painted lips curved into an encouraging smile, and you took me into your arms as the first slow dance played. It was old, familiar to me as your body was against mine: Zeppelin's D'yer Mak'er.

The room melted from my vision. I could still feel the bodies pressed in close — the heat of so many others dancing nearby, the perfume of so many females crowded together — but mentally, I was in my own world with you. Watching was breathtaking: the pulse in the hollow of your throat, your lipsticked mouth curving into a smile. I was anxious to smear the glossy red from your lips, desperate suddenly to kiss it all away.

Couldn't wait to get you home, couldn't wait another beat. I had to kiss you. My mouth met yours and instantly I found pure delight. Your mouth opened on mine and drank me in. Your lipstick was waxy-tasting, and it slid from your mouth. There was something false in the flavor, manufactured of course, but there was also something sexual in the fact that I was already undressing you. By removing your lipstick, I was uncovering the real woman apparent beneath the society shell.

It made me think to the future, how I would lovingly remove every trace of makeup from your face. How I would undress you, wash you, spread you out before me and drink you in.

We danced in circles, moving in tighter and tighter. Your breath was redolent of the alcohol, but again, the scent beneath that was purely your own. Familiar to me. As I kissed you again, I suddenly knew what it would be like to taste you, to kneel down and set my head against your thigh, breathing in deeply to catch the waves of your own private scent.

"I'm yours," you whispered to me, your soft hand coming up to stroke my cheek, grazing on my five o'clock shadow. You turned my face so that I was looking directly into your eyes, and you kissed me once the words were barely out of your mouth, your tongue parting my lips as you drank from me. I gripped your slender waist and let myself respond, my mind on hold, my thoughts stopped dead like a candle snuffed by a sudden puff of air.

Sputter. Flicker. Gone.

Your kisses were silver-hot and pure. Each movement you made was one of ownership, claiming me: your mouth on mine, your hands in my hair, your fingers on the back of my neck. I suddenly feel like an over-sexed teenager all over again, waiting to make that move for a first kiss in the fading light of a summer day.

You took me by the hand then—still giving me that gentle, reassuring smile accompanied by a squeeze with your fingertips—and you led me through the multitude of dancing partners to one of the unisex rest rooms. The bathrooms at this club each have separate doors covered with pictures of sexy movie stars, sirens: Kathleen Turner, Linda Hamilton, Meg Tilly, a medley of lovely faces beaming down at us. You chose the third door and pulled me through it, turning the knob so that a sign appeared on the reverse side: occupied.

The room surprised me, the marble-topped sink and counter, huge round mirror from the 20s, blue-tinted mirrored walls. The walls and mirror allowed for a two-way reflection—our images were doubled and tripled to infinity. A wooden clothes rack stood to one side of the door, and a padded bench ran the length of the room.

While I watched, you pulled off your jersey dress and then came into my arms. We could still hear the music from the dance floor, and now, in the soft light of the private bathroom, we danced alone, the blue-tinged mirrored walls sending multiple images of our entwined bodies moving slowly together, that first-kiss feeling of naked skin on skin.

Watch us from above for an out of body experience. I slowly undo the straps on your slip and pull the little flit of fabric from your body. I kiss my way along the ridges of your shoulders, the collarbones, the naked hollow of your neck—avoiding your breasts—down your belly, your hips, skipping your pussy as I head for your knees, back of your calves, ankles, insteps, toes.

I kiss you slowly, lingering each step of the way. You start to shake as I begin the journey back, kissing just as slowly, just as gently, the indents at the backs of your knees, the tender skin at your inner thighs, and then, without hesitating or changing your rhythm, I press my face to your pussy.

I am sure they can hear your moan on the dance floor, am certain that you sigh loud enough for people to come and see what is wrong. But I don't stop, don't even look up at you as I continue working.

I spread your pussy lips and lap and lick over your clit. Hungry, so hungry. You lose you fingers in my hair, twirl and tease them in

my hair. You say my name in a husky whisper, say it louder as my
circles go faster and stronger.

No, I'm wrong now, thinking back. I lied before. It didn't
start last night. It didn't start when I first shook your hand.
It started before I ever met you. I was waiting for you. I know
this now, your body so carefully wrapped around my own. I
was waiting for you, and you were waiting for me.

My tongue continued its magic trip until you came. And
then you immediately took over from my position.

Watch us now. Watch me lean against the sink, gripping tightly
with both hands. I am out of control, you can tell by my shattered
breathing, by the pulse that jumps and dances in my throat.
I'm so high, I can't make a sound. Not a moan. Not a sigh. I am
frozen, feeling, dying for you to make it happen.
Yes, that's the way, that's the way. The cool tile of the sink, my
fingers tightening, almost painfully, gripping the porcelain. That's
you down there, the sweet red-haired firecracker drinking me down.

But that was last night. And now it's morning, and you
are curled, kittenlike, in my arms, breathing in that deep,
rhythmic way that signifies bliss.
Total bliss.
And I stroke your hair, and I lay my hand palm-down on
the nape of your neck to feel your warmth. And I look long
and hard at you as I realize it doesn't matter when it started,
only that it began at all.

Overnight Train

"Est-ce que je peux partager ce compartiment avec vous?"
Your accent's so bad, I almost can't understand you.
You're pretty—strikingly pretty, in fact, and very French-
looking. Not that I know what "French looking" means, but
there's a certain style I've come to expect in French women,
and you embody it—despite the American accent coming
out of your pretty lips as you form the words, nervously.
Maybe it's the too-tight T-shirt that deceives me. But then I
see the ring in your nose, the plain outline of nipple rings.
You're American—no doubt about that; it would be obvious,
even if it wasn't for the dyed-black bob or the Einsturzende
Neubaten logo on your white T-shirt, its face distorted by
the swell of your full breasts and the firm buds of your nipples
and nipple rings. Then again, you could pass for German if
your French was better. The short black skirt looks more like
Europe than Berkeley—and the black knee-high Doc Martens,
could more properly be called Doc Maartens. The piercings
might be explained by your being a Berliner.

But you're American—of that, I have no doubt
whatsoever. You're that unique brand of American traveler,
I suppose, American Eurotrash, emulating the glamour of
the continent, compelled to explore it in—what, your Junior
year of college? Shortly after graduation? I sigh, remembering
my first trip to Europe, two years ago, decked out in Tour De
France shirts and Nina Hagen buttons. What cynics we
become in a couple short years.

We've just left the train station in some small French
village, and you've just boarded, from the look of your heavy

army-surplus backpack, looking only slightly less fashionable than your skirt, boots, and piercings.

I notice with some interest that your tight T-shirt has pulled up above your belly button, revealing another piercing and the faint twist of a modern-primitives tattoo: stylized black ivy, mingled with barbed wire.

"*Est-ce que je peux partager ce compartiment avec vous? Vous? Partager? Ce Compartiment?*"

Meekly, you stare at me, eyes wide. I see the look of desperation and the way you're studying the English-French phrase book, and your prettiness is lost in weeks of Paris in June, running into clueless Americans and helping them order baguettes. If it wasn't 9:00 on the night train to Berlin, after a long day of corporate bullshit, I would probably be friendlier, say: "I speak English," maybe even say "I'm American," rather than faking a French accent, which I do occasionally when I'm trying to avoid too much bonding with my Hawaiian-shirted countrymen. Certainly I don't look like an American tourist at this point—I had to rush to the Paris train station from my job interview with an obnoxious Texas oil millionaire who treated me like shit. I'm wearing an expensive suit, rumpled from several hours on the train.

"*Oui,*" I say. "S'il vous plait, prenez un siège."

You look like a deer in French headlights. You glance from me to your phrase book, then back again.

"I'm sorry," you say. "I don't speak French. *Parlais vous Anglais?*"

I sigh, wrestling with my conscience. You're very cute, but it's very late, and I've had about all the Americanisms I can take for the day.

"No," I say.

"Oh, well," you say. You take the seat opposite me in the otherwise empty compartment. You begin to rummage through your bag for something to read.

The lights are low outside, but we've both got reading lights on. I had been about to turn mine out and try to get some sleep, but now I'm a little reluctant to do that. Part of it is your pretty face, full of possibility, just a couple of years younger than me but seeming so different in attitude. But the most part is that I feel guilty for lying to you, for pretending to be French when you no doubt, traveling alone, would have loved to connect with a fellow Yank.

So I sit there pretending to read a French magazine, though the best I can manage is to look at the pictures. It always stuns me how much nudity they have in French publications; I realize as I look over the pictures of slim French models that I haven't been with a woman on this whole trip— three months of denial, overwork and sublimation. And it doesn't help that when I look up, you're stretching—your back arched, your lithe body twisted in its seat, your breasts straining against the too-tight shirt, your black bra showing plainly through the thin white fabric, damp with your sweat. Your eyes are closed and as you enjoy your stretch—making it look almost yoga-inspired—your face looks lost in an expression of rapture, an almost-sexual abandon.

My eyes rove over you, taking in the paleness of your belly, the intricacy of your tattoos, the way your short skirt rides up on your thighs, showing the tops of your black lace stockings and the garters they attach to. Very punk-rock. And more than a little enticing. Your knees are slightly apart and I can almost see up your skirt; I'm sure, after running for the train, you're unaware that you're almost flashing me. You're lost in the delight of your much-needed stretch.

Except that when you open your eyes, you catch me. Staring at you, the hunger no doubt plain on my face.

And instead of looking angry, you smile. I expect, for a moment, that you'll wink, but perhaps you think better of it. You don't look away; you keep staring, even as my face grows hot, telling me that you know you've embarrassed me.

"Pardon," I mumble, looking down.

You don't answer. Instead, you stand up and bend over your backpack, unpacking its contents on the seat. In fact, it could be my imagination, but I think you bend over just a bit further than you need to. This time I really can't take my eyes off you—it's not a choice, it's an overwhelming compulsion, as you reel me in with the American brashness I've grown so accustomed to—but not in this way. Why do women never do this to me at home?

God, you're wearing a thong. As you bend over, I see your tight skirt pulling against the thin strap between your rounded cheeks. I can even see the top of it at the hem, a black lace thong that doesn't look like it has much to it.

Very European, I want to tell you, but I resist the urge and instead watch as you bend over still further, refraining from kneeling down, which would no doubt give you better access to the contents of your pack. Instead, you bend very far forward, your thighs slightly parted, your shirt riding up your back so I can see the full mounds of your breasts hanging invitingly. I take a deep breath and realize I can smell you in the small compartment—the sharpness of female sweat, of a college student spending weeks on the road with long hours in trains filled up with thoughts of sex. The scent is so sexy it hurts me to inhale it. I feel my cock stirring in my suit pants. I drape the magazine in my lap, staring as you find what you were looking for. You've got a makeup mirror, now, and you're fumbling with it as the train rocks you back and forth suggestively.

You're putting on lipstick.

But you're not finished with me. You reach behind you and make a show of gently tugging at the strap of your thong, as if it were possible for me to miss your sexy underwear. You sit back down and wait a full beat before glancing up.

This time, you catch me, but I don't look away. You lock eyes with me, smile mischievously, and bite the tip of your finger. You're wearing bright red lipstick, what an ex-girlfriend used to call "cocksucker red." My heart pounds in my chest, and I'm finding it hard to breathe.

Your lips wrap around the tip of your finger as you chew at your nail. I don't take my eyes off you—even if you're a clueless coquette unaware of the effect she's having on me, I don't care. My eyes are hungry for you, desperate to drink in your body. If you were going to be offended by my looking, you would have already left the compartment.

So I look, and I'm so bewitched by the way you're chewing your nail that it takes me several long minutes to realize what book you're reading.

It's not that I recognize that specific book, certainly. But I recognize its *type*. The portrait of a nymphet, skimpily-clad, on the cover. A slightly suggestive title, perhaps: "Stranger's Kiss"—suggestive to its American audience, at least. It could pass for a romance novel—if I hadn't read them myself.

You're reading a porn novel.

Now my cock is fully hard; it hurts, having been soft for so many weeks of neglect as I searched for consultant work in Belgium, France and Germany. But it's coming back to full form, and feeling the pulse of my blood fill it makes me want you more than I've ever wanted any woman.

I pretend to read my magazine, but each of the slim French models now bears your face, stripped naked before my eyes and beckoning to me.

When the conductor comes by, I have to reach in my jacket pocket for my ticket. The magazine slides off my lap, and when I look up from grabbing it, I see your eyes locked firmly on my crotch. There's no mistaking the telltale bulge under the thin dress slacks. The conductor notices it, too. He looks from me to you to me again, and raises his eyebrow.

"*Merci*," he says as he gives me back my punched ticket.

You lean back in your seat, your legs stretched out, your knees now parted. God, now I can almost see up your skirt again. The smooth, creamy skin of your pale thighs makes me want to drop something again, get an excuse to look right up to your panties—your thong, the skimpy black thong I caught a glimpse of earlier.

You chew on your red-painted nail and engross yourself in your book, like you're savoring every morsel of it. I squint, trying to read the copy on the back of the book. All I can make out are a few scattered phrases—"penchant for spanking," "anonymous lust," "untenable desire." And, toward the bottom, "becomes a shameless slut."

When you glance up over the edge of your book, you see me reading the back, and you smile. Are you teasing me, or are you looking for a stranger's kiss, like your cheesy book? Paralyzed by my own desire and the slow rocking of the train, I try to breathe deep and wait for the next move of the chess piece in this game of seduction we're playing.

It's not long before the train stops, and we wait for customs. The officer comes by and you give him your passport. Without thinking, I give him mine as well.

When I look back at you, you're staring at me, the edges of your lips twisted in a nasty smile.

"Tsk, tsk," you utter.

I realize with a rush of embarrassment that you saw my passport cover. You know I'm an American.

I sit there, silent, for long minutes, my face growing many shades of red. It takes me awhile to realize that you've returned to your provocative reading position—slouched in your seat, legs slightly parted, tempting me to look. When you stretch, I see your nipples poking hard through the white T-shirt. You look at me, pointedly, and then go back to reading your book.

"I don't blame you," you sigh. "A lot of American girls are really charmed by French men. No wonder you'd pretend to be French to charm a naive Yankee girl. Maybe you were just trying to get a little American booty?"

"Well," I begin, but I can't find anything to say.

You laugh. "But I guess the deception's over for me, too, isn't it? You know what I'm reading."

"I'm sorry," I say. "It isn't like that—I've just been dealing with so many Americans lately."

You fix my eyes with yours, and your smile's pretty but cruel.

"Assholes, aren't they?"

"You can say that again."

"Well, I reserve judgment. Everybody's an asshole when they're traveling. Isn't that right?"

This time your smile is disarming, even friendly.

I start to introduce myself, but you put up your hand.

"Please," you say. "I'd prefer to think of you as 'Frenchy.'"

I blush. "And your name?"

You look at me suspiciously.

"Mmmm…no, Frenchy, I don't think so. After all, you're American. There are a lot of stalkers in America, aren't there? You seem like the obsessive type."

I redden still more, but you smile and lean even further back in your seat, your knees parting just a bit further. Now, there's no mistaking it—I can see up your skirt, to the tiny patch of black lace caressing your pussy. I find myself wondering if you're pierced there, too. I can't take my eyes off of you, and when you glance up you see that I'm staring, shamelessly, up your skirt. I look into your eyes and there's a hunger there, accented by the way you lick your cocksucker-red lips.

"There's nothing wrong with a little American booty," you say. "I've even been known to indulge myself."

That's all I need. I stand up, go to the compartment door, and lock it. I pull the curtains and turn back toward you. Now you're leaned all the way down in your seat, your legs spread, a smile on your face.

I pick up your backpack, place it on my seat. I take the seat next to you and you wriggle upright. You toss your book onto your backpack and turn halfway toward me.

Your lips and tongue taste like clove cigarettes, and you thrust deep into my mouth as we kiss. I put my arms around you and you melt into me, pressing your body against mine. I can feel the firm peaks of your nipples with their metal rings, your breasts bobbing gently against my chest as we kiss hungrily. You bring your legs up across my thighs, leaning against the wall and pulling me closer.

I can feel your thigh rubbing my cock. You slip your hands under my jacket and help me slip it off. I unknot my tie; you pull it and toss it across the small compartment. It's warm outside, and it's getting warmer in here. You start to unbutton my shirt as your breathing quickens.

I pull up your shirt, finding your black bra snugged down over your nipples. There's not much to it to begin with—it's really a demi-bra, with stiff padding to lift and separate your breasts. You don't seem to need it, though; as my fingertips caress your tits, I find them firm, just as I doubt you need the rings in your nipples to keep them hard; still, it all gives you an exotic flair, like someone you'd meet on the overnight train to Berlin.

You moan softly as I caress your breasts. You get my shirt open and slide it over my shoulders. It falls sweat-limp to the floor of the compartment. I bend forward and my lips find your nipples, tugging the lace cups of your bra down further so I can suckle you into my mouth. My free hand plays with your other nipple, listening to you whimper as I pinch slightly harder. Your hand slides between your own legs and down to my crotch; you stroke my hard cock as the motions of the train rock us slowly back and forth against each other.

I undo the front clasp of your bra, peeling the material off of your breasts. You reach down and take hold of your skin-tight T-shirt, lifting it off and tossing it away. I lean forward and kiss you hard, our tongues mingling as our upper bodies, now bare, slide easily together on a thin film of perspiration.

"Have you ever fucked a stranger before?" you whisper to me.

"No," I say. "I don't think so."

"You're about to," you say, and start to unfasten my belt.

Now it's my turn to lean back in the seat, as far as I can go, as you drop to your knees between my spread legs and make short work of my belt and zipper. My cock has been hurting since the first moment you entered the compartment—it's been hurting, wanting you.

Your cocksucker-red lips descend on my cock, and you slurp me into your mouth, whimpering softly as you swallow me. Your tongue swirls around the head and your lips clamp tightly over the shaft, your head bobbing slowly up and down as I run my fingers through your bobbed black hair. I'm moaning, not caring if other passengers hear me—the walls on these compartments are notoriously thin, but I couldn't quiet my moans if I tried. You're a genius with that pretty mouth of yours—or maybe you just want me so bad you can't help yourself. Your lips and tongue are all over me, up and down my shaft, swirling around the head as it leaks pre-come into your mouth, making you suck me harder. Your fingertips graze my balls and your sharp fingernails toy with my sensitive flesh. Your other hand travels up my chest, pinching first one nipple and then the other as you suck my cock eagerly.

I'm getting closer—terribly close, in fact. I can feel your mouth enveloping my cock, threatening to bring me off and suck the come right out of me, without thought to my pleasure. You're feeding, devouring what you want whether or not it wants to be taken. My hips rock in time with the thrusts of your mouth, and you can tell I'm getting very close.

You pull your mouth off of me with obvious difficulty, panting, your tongue and lips still working as if of their own volition. You look up at me, your lipstick smeared half across your face and half across my cock.

"I want you to come in my mouth," you pant. "But can you get hard again?"

"I don't think that'll be a problem," I tell you. I haven't even finished saying it before you're on me again, your fingers wrapped around the base of my shaft, your head pumping desperately, not taking no for an answer. The tight suction of your mouth pulls me along inexorably toward my orgasm, as does the surging heat of your tongue against the underside of my cockhead. When my ass comes thrusting off the seat, you know it's coming, and I hear a desirous moan deep in your throat as you wait for it, hungry, demanding.

Then I feel the first spasm, and you suckle eagerly at my cock as I fill your mouth. Another spasm, and you suck just as hard, swallowing before I even know I've finished coming. You look up at me, your lips now slick, your eyes dancing and sparkling.

A smile twists your lips, and you lick them.

"You've been watching it all night," you whisper. "I want to see if you need it as bad as you think you do."

You stand up, your body looking glorious in the yellow light of the compartment. I watch, bewitched, as you slide your fingers under the elastic waist of your skirt and wriggle it down over your hips. As it reaches your thighs, it falls, descending to your booted feet, leaving your pussy clad only in the skimpy thong that entranced me in the first place. You've shaved quite close—there isn't a hint of pubic hair.

You kick the discarded skirt away and turn around, leaning over so I can feel your ass. You've got several more tattoos, ranging in suggestiveness from a red rose on your butt to a naked go-go dancer on the back of your upper thigh. I take hold of your thong and pull it down, smelling the fullness of your pussy as the wet material peels off of you.

It's soaked through.

The tiny thong falls to your ankles and you kick it away. Now you're nude except for your knee-high boots, and when you climb into my lap I smell your pussy so strong that I'm overcome with lust for it.

I guide you back into your seat, into the seat where you teased me for hours, perhaps deciding if you were going to fuck me or not. Now your legs spread all the way, smoothly, easily, your creamy thighs inviting me in a much more decisive way. I get on my knees and press my face between your legs, feeling it against your pussy.

It's not just trimmed—it's smooth, utterly smooth. *Must be hard to maintain in hostels*, I think. The feel of a shaved pussy is new to me, and it excites me to have my tongue running against silken flesh. As I lick your pussy lips, you gasp, breathing slowly. I tease your lips open and expose the firm bud of your entrance, glistening with moisture and begging me to savor it.

My tongue finds your pussy and I lick hungrily.

Now it's your turn to moan—loudly, uncontrollably. Your pussy is strong, tangy. Its taste is intense, but it only makes me want more. My tongue traces a path around your entrance, savoring your juice as I realize how incredibly wet you are. Maybe you *weren't* deciding whether or not to fuck me—maybe you had decided to fuck whoever you found in this compartment, no matter who he was—or she.

I draw my tongue up to your clit, finding the unfamiliar heat of stainless steel. A small ring, piercing the hood of your clitoris—something I've never experienced. I suckle your clit and your clit ring into my mouth, the tip of my tongue flickering over it as your thighs come tightly closed around my face, your nude body writhing in pleasure. My hands move up and find your full breasts, pinching the nipples and caressing them as I eat you out. I've never tasted anything so delicious in my life—and I want more of it. I lick down to your opening again and I can almost feel the juices gushing out, flowing onto my tongue, feeding me as my come fed you.

I return to your clit, pinching your nipples harder with my fingers. Your moans grow louder as I center in on your pierced bud, feeling like a lion with its prey—or is it the other way around?

I hear your moans heightening, like you're moving quickly toward your orgasm. Your hands have come to rest on mine, holding them on your breasts as if to beg me not to stop—or to warn me against stopping. In response, I pinch harder, and the slow thrust of your hips forcing your pussy onto my face becomes a quick one, then a blur of motion as you pump your cunt against my mouth.

Lost in the taste of your pussy, the feel of your thighs around my face, the smells of your body overwhelming me, I almost don't realize how hard I've become.

It's so rare for me to get hard right after coming. I have no idea how many minutes it's been since I came in your mouth, but the fact that my cock throbs with hunger for you tells me how much you turn me on—as if I didn't already know. I'm quite sure you'd let me fuck you any moment now. I'm quite sure if I sat up, pushed your legs onto my shoulders and fucked you, you'd beg for more. But I'm not finished with you yet—I want to savor every taste, every feeling that your cunt has to offer, so I lick down to your entrance once more and thrust my tongue in, as far as it will go, hearing you moan still louder and feeling you writhe against me as you strive to push your crotch harder against my face.

"Fuck me," you beg. "Fuck me right now."

I lift my face to yours, and you kiss me open-mouthed though I'm still dripping your juices. You reach down and find my cock hard, breathing a sigh of relief. But you don't guide it to your cunt, don't push it inside yourself. You asked me to fuck you, and you want to *be* fucked.

So, without my hands, I nuzzle the head of my cock into your pussy.

You're so slick, I could go in easily. The head of my cock finds your entrance without the slightest effort. But I tug it up slightly, teasing your clit, feeling the ring against the head of my cock. Your hands lay inert at your sides, letting me take control. You look up at me, moaning softly, an almost-sob of desperation. Your eyes are wide, and you look like you're almost in tears from wanting my cock.

"Fuck me," you whimper. "Please? Please fuck me?"

I can't resist any more. With just the slightest adjustment of my hips, my cockhead slides down from your clit and back between your pussy lips, to the swollen entrance of your cunt.

Your eyes are locked in mine, begging. Desperate. Hungry.

"Please?" you whimper. "Please fuck me?"

I push into you in a single thrust, going all the way in without pause. Your eyes go wide, your mouth pops open, and you begin to shake. At first I think I've hurt you, but then your arms are around me, pulling me hard against you, our bodies slicking together in the sweat, your breath choking in your throat. You're coming, coming desperately, uncontrollably, and I can feel the spasms of your cunt around the shaft of my cock. I slide out and thrust in again, and your body tenses and arches against me as you shove against me, meeting my hard thrust with your own. I start to fuck you rhythmically, and your orgasm fades into soft moans of ecstasy as I give you my cock in thrust after thrust with the head firmly nudging your cervix at the terminus of each thrust.

I slide out of you, my hard cock glistening with your pussy. I can smell you strong in the tiny compartment, and I want to fuck you for as long as I can, in every way I can.

Our eyes meet, and you seem to realize in an instant why I've pulled out of you.

"Oh God," you whisper. "Are you going to fuck me from behind?"

I'm about to say "If you want me to," but it's quite clear that the mere recitation of your phrase has turned you on even more. "You're going to fuck me from behind," you whisper. "You're going to fuck me doggy-style."

"What could be more American?" I say.

You slide off the seat, bending yourself over the edge of it, stretched with your ass thrust high in the air. You spread your legs and look back at me.

"Well now that you mention it," you say. "We've had French already. We may as well try Greek."

I look at you, and you raise your eyebrows, smiling.

"You're serious?" I ask.

"Uh-huh," you say, nodding. You nod toward your bag. "The outside compartment."

You kneel there, ass raised high, legs spread, pussy and asshole displayed gorgeously for my use. I find the small bottle of lubricant and return. Your hips are gently rocking back and forth as you wait for me to slide my cock back into you.

Your pussy is moist, almost dripping with desire. I

snuggle up behind you and my cockhead finds it again; I enter you with a gentle thrust, this time, and you push back onto me, moaning softly. In this position you can move much better, and you start working yourself onto my cock rhythmically, fucking your pussy over my shaft as I pop the lid of the lubricant and drizzle a short stream between your cheeks.

You gasp, then whimper softly as I find your asshole with my thumb. I start to fuck you easily, and now you don't thrust back. You hold still, letting me take control, letting me have you. I rub your asshole gently open; then, almost effortlessly, my thumb pops in.

"God, that feels good," you moan.

"Are you sure you want to do this?"

"I'm experiencing Europe to the fullest," you tell me.

I slide my cock out of your pussy and drizzle more lube over the head of my cock. You reach back and part your cheeks, holding them open for me. I adjust my posture just enough to get the right angle into your rear entrance. I nuzzle the head of my cock against your asshole and almost immediately you push back against me.

"Yes," you whisper. "It feels good."

With a slow, even thrust, I enter your ass. Your whole body goes rigid for an instant, and I think at first that you can't take it, that you over-estimated your receptivity back there. But then you're moaning, whispering "Fuck me" over and over again, and I start to pump into your ass, lifted high on one knee, entering you easier and easier with each thrust as you open up. Your hand has slid between your legs and now you're rubbing your clit, rapidly, your moans louder than ever as I thrust into your ass.

"I'm going to come again," you choke, and then I feel the spasms again, this time so different, your asshole around my cock, milking me. "Fuck me harder," you gasp, with great effort through the intensity of your orgasm, and I fuck faster, deeper, taking every inch of your asshole as I mount toward my own orgasm. When I reach it, you're still coming, your nude body shuddering and writhing against the seat as you pump yourself back onto me. The pleasure pulses through my body as I let myself go deep inside your ass.

When I slide out of you, you slump onto the floor and sigh, looking up at me.

"American booty," you say. "Nothing like it."

I'm asleep in the seats, wrapped around you when the train rolls to a stop in whatever town you're going to. While you extricate yourself from my grasp, I pretend I'm still asleep. I guess I've never liked awkward goodbyes.

You scrawl out a note and leave it tucked under my rumpled jacket. I read it as soon as you've closed the compartment door behind you.

Frenchy:
Here's my number at home—in case you ever make it to the States. I know it's a long trip, but perhaps you'll drop by some day. If you do call, just tell my roommate it's Frenchy.

You've signed it with a smiley face with devil horns—and no name.

I take a deep breath of the close air in the compartment, smelling all the different parts of you.

"Vive le Frenchy," I mumble to myself, and go back to sleep.

Deep Inside You

You were the one and only girlfriend I missed after we'd broken up. Others haven't even left an echo of sadness lingering after their departure—and maybe that says something about my romantic choices—but you have stayed with me over the years. Memories of you. Images of us together. Look, I know all about why we broke up. It made perfect sense at the time. We'd been too young to stay together, that was the only flaw in our relationship. You said that you wanted to experience more before settling down. I was too unstable to try and convince you to stay. And it's probably a good thing that I let you go. For both of our sakes. If I'd held you down, you wouldn't have been happy being with me. You wouldn't have been happy at all.

Now, that I'm in my thirties (and we'll just leave it at that), I've realized how much I loved you. You were the perfect counterpart to my calm, quiet personality. You were energetic, emotional, easy for people to approach. I'm severe looking, methodical in my actions, slow to become riled. Together, we made up the ideal person. You were able to bring me out of my shell. I worked to keep you focused, directed on where you wanted to go.

Since my latest unhappy breakup, I've thought a lot about you, have toyed with the idea of trying to find you. I'd decided to treat this time on my own differently than my past behaviors. Usually, following the demise of a relationship, I've thrown myself into the dating scene. I've staked out dance clubs, renewed acquaintances with the bevy of beautiful bartenders in our city, done the circuit. A warm body in my bed was better than *no*body, I thought. In fact, that's how most guys think, right?

Now, my mind focused on you, I became more of a recluse. Went to the gym to get out my aggressions. Went for a run when I needed the extra release of my feet pounding hard on the pavement. And when the need for sex arose powerfully within me (as it does for any healthy man), I rented porno movies. And there... in the least likely place of all, I found you, my naughty ex-love.

Who would have thought? That was my first question. Was this what you meant when you said you wanted to go out and see the world?

You were in a rather slick flick, not totally sleazy like some, but still, X-rated. You looked gorgeous, as always, your long, honey-colored hair cut to a chin-length bob, your white teeth gleaming beneath the lights as you grinned before sinking your mouth into some slut's pussy. I was enraptured. I'd always wanted to get the two of us on tape, but hadn't ever gone through with it. Now, I was able to watch you as you did all the delightful, sensuous things we'd done when we were together—except you were doing them with another woman. How fucking awesome was that? My first instinct was deluded pride. It was in my head to call up my buddies and invite them over to watch—to brag about having been with you and *now* look at you! It would have won me a lot of cache with the guys.

But somehow that seemed unfaithful to you. Crazy, right? Here you were, enjoying a medley of pleasures at the hands of another—

Oh, wait... Two other lovers. Just look at that. You and the other girl, and now a third, joining you all. I almost lost it right then.

What really rocked my world was when you took two ladies on at once. Wearing a strap-on, you fucked a blonde missionary style while a petite Asian girl, also wearing a strap-on, plunged her cock into your backdoor. This was too pretty for words, my ex-love, a perky, slender thing, becoming a "triple-girl sandwich" between two other beauties.

It was actually too much for me to take. All of my worries, my nervousness about calling you, disappeared. But how was I supposed to get a hold of you? It had literally been years since we last talked. Still, I dug up my old address book, and I dialed your old number, not thinking I'd have much luck but unable to figure out how else to start. To my delight, I got your roommate, ex-roommate now, who forwarded me to a new number. I dialed that with trembling hands, sure to get a machine. Instead, I got you.

You sounded warm and sleepy, and I envisioned you curled up in bed, book in hand, cup of tea by the side of the bed. Perhaps you were in the living room, sipping a glass of sherry while you watched some old black-and-white movie on television. Or, maybe, you were in bed with a lover, whose cock was deep inside you, a lover with a nasty side who wanted to watch you try to keep up a conversation while getting fucked. That was a better image—I actually liked the thought of it, even if I did feel immediately jealous of the fictitious person I'd created in my head.

"I saw you in your film debut," I said, without stating my name. You'd know my voice. If you didn't, then it wasn't meant to be, was it? "Nice touch, when the third girl entered the scene."

"Hey, you," you said, and I could hear the smile in your voice.

"So, how'd you get into all that?"

There was a hesitation, as if you thought I might be judging you. But then you correctly figured out the question was simply one out of curiosity. Who am I to judge what you have to do, right? I've done plenty of things in the past that you know about and that you could judge me for. After a moment, you laughed lightly and said, "I just did the one. Sort of for a dare. I wanted to know if I could, and I chose my friends to do it with, so there wasn't anything scary about it. We made a nice little packet of money, too. So what did you really think?" you asked.

"That you looked like an angel."

"And?"

"That I wished it was me in the video with you. Wished it was me in real life with you."

"You don't think it was a bad move?"

"How could I say that?" I asked, "it helped me find you."

Then you sighed and, in that dreamy way of yours, you whispered, "I really miss you."

That was all I needed. I confessed how turned on I'd been at seeing your movie, and begged for you to let me see you again. There wasn't even a pause on your part. You gave me the address, a condo off Sunset, and told me you'd be ready when I arrived.

You were ready. Oh, man, were you ready. You greeted me naked, showing off your amazing body by doing a quick spin before letting me in the door. Then, without a word, you took me to your balcony. Looking down at Hollywood below us, at the lights of all the hopeful starlets, I plunged into you over and over with my rock-like cock. You gripped the bannister while I worked you, stepping up on your tiptoes to offer me the best access from behind. You were so very wet, and your pussy made a nice, welcoming smacking sound as it enveloped my cock with each stroke.

"I missed you, too," I murmured, pressing my lips against the back of your neck, breathing in deeply to catch a whiff of your scent, the fragrance of your skin beneath the heady wash of Chanel #5. The wave of your scent washed over me, bathing me in memories from twelve years before, when we were both much younger, much more innocent.

But now, fucking the sweet, satiny pussy of my lovely ex-, I realized that the time we'd had away had only made this meeting more divine. That our new shot at the relationship was strengthened by our age. I whispered this to you, as you leaned your lovely body against mine, rubbing your hips up and down, doing all the work now, fucking me instead of letting me fuck you.

Man, I missed this. Our bodies always worked so well together, didn't they? Mine seemed to fit perfectly within yours. And the way you squeezed and released on me let me know exactly how close you were to coming. I've never been as in tune with any other woman.

I stroked your full round breasts as we fucked, cradled the weight of them in the palms of my hands. My body tingled as I remembered each line and curve of your body. I'd fantasies about this for a dozen years. Doing it again was almost like living out a dirty daydream.

"Oh, yes," you agreed, coming on my cock, your voice growing louder as you climaxed. "Yes, oh, yes, oh, yes," a sinfully sexy mantra that echoed into the glittering town of Hollywood below us.

"Yesssss!" you screamed as I took over and rammed it home...

...deep inside you.

The Exhibit

Everyone was talking about you. Let's start with that simple fact. Everyone was discussing you as if you were the next big thing. You know that way people talk. That knowing way they have when relating gossip or other forms of hearsay.

"Have you heard? Isn't she *great*?"

"Oh, yes. The next Matisse."

"Really? I thought more Modigliani—"

Speaking in that faux stage whisper, a hushed in-awe tone. It seemed for a little while that every time I turned around, someone was saying your name.

"She's just great," they'd gush. They spoke of your signature red lips and the avant-garde way you had of looking down at people as you spoke, as if you were standing up on a pedestal and the rest of us were tiny ants, crawling on the floor below. Artists who are in the spotlight can behave like you. That's part of the package. And art enthusiasts, patrons willing to fork over hundreds of times what a piece of art is worth, seem to like being treated badly by the artists.

Don't ask me why this is. I don't know. I can only assume it follows the same unspoken rule that people will think something is more valuable if it is more expensive. Most of us know that this is not always the case. But if you take the same two sweaters, price one at $300 and the other at $30, there is a group of women who will buy the $300 and give you reason after reason why it is better quality than it's identical, cheaper counterpart.

I have to say, that in my opinion your artwork fell into this category. Your pieces were average, as far as I could tell.

An interested collector could find a match for your work at any local art college. But someone, some doddering patron, had decided that you were an up-and-coming somebody. And this person single-handedly got you a showing where other patrons, like those characters who watched in breathless awe as the Emperor paraded in his new clothes, walked around the gallery *oohing* and *ahhing* and writing out multi-thousand dollar checks.

Sure, maybe I was prejudiced against you. I hate when people tell me that I'm going to love something. Like *Titanic*—oh, you'll love it. In truth? I couldn't sit through the stupid thing. Or steak tartar—oooh, so delicious. You must try it! Really? To me, it looks like a whole lot of raw beef. So that was my mental state when I went to see your work in person rather than just the prints I'd witnessed in the catalog.

At the show, the buzz of the crowd centered on the fact that your work was different. Unique. That you had created your paintings in an altogether previously unheard of manner. All right, I must admit that the concept piqued my interest, and, as critic for one of the country's most respected papers (I won't toot my own horn by telling you which one), I answered "yes" to my invitation and attended the show.

I'd met you before, and you were just as bland to me in person as you'd been in the gossip. It's fine if you laugh now. I'm telling you how it was for me then. But as I walked around the gallery, studying the paintings, I tried to figure out what it was about them that made them so truly different. I was startled to find myself falling under the same spell of fawning art lovers that I so detest. And yet, there was something, something that had not shown up in the reproductions I had seen, that had not been captured by the photographs.

I moved closer, until my nose was nearly against one of the paintings, and then, just then, I felt a body next to mine. You know all about timing, and you had moved stealthily into my personal space and had pressed your ruby-glossed lips to my ear. I felt the tickle of your breath and it sent a shiver straight down my spine. I have to tell you now, that I was hard in an instant, and I worked to keep up my blase attitude. My back stiffened, and I held entirely still as you were whispering, "I have a secret... should I share it?"

"Secret?" I responded. "Why would you want to tell me?"

"You know," you said. "That burning urge to confess—"

Harder still. Let me say now. Those words made me harder than a pole. I wanted to turn and grab you in my arms, to stare in your eyes and insist that you do just that: confess. Forget the art world, this was exactly the type of discussion suited to my libido. But we were in public, among peers, and I simply said, "Confess."

Then your hand was in my own, leading me to the back of the gallery, to the private office of the gallery owner. And you were locking the door behind you and moving again into my space, so close that I had to keep myself from stepping back.

"I mix something special with my paints," you said. "A pure ingredient. The purest, really."

I felt a deep letdown in my expectations. From your actions in the gallery, I had thought you were going to tell me about your sexual desires, your kinky needs to have wild, animal sex with every art journalist you saw. Wouldn't that have been good luck? As it was, I squinted my eyes at you, trying to read what you might silently be hoping to tell me. There was something so peculiar about you. Perhaps, this is why people kept talking. You didn't look like anyone I'd ever seen before. Couldn't compare you to a movie star or known celebrity. You had your own appeal.

Your golden hair shined oddly beneath the lights and your lips, in that bizarre shade of red, turned upward in a bewitching smile, transforming your face into one of ethereal beauty. While I watched, in stunned silence, you removed your dress, then your undergarments, then spread yourself out on the floor and began to masturbate. To my total amazement, you continued to speak to me as you worked yourself, your fingers disappearing into the slit between your legs, your hips rising and falling on the cool, marble floor.

"I mix this special, secret substance with my paints. And somehow, for some reason, people think my paintings are remarkably beautiful, almost addictive to look at. They have a magical shine to them..."

And all the while you were talking, those slender hips of yours were bucking against the floor. From my vantage point, I could see your shaved pussylips, their pale pink skin richer and darker on the inside. Your fingers moved rapidly, up and down, and then you began using two together to impale yourself. I wanted to do that for you. Not with my fingers, but with my cock. If you had made any gesture to me, I would have, first getting down between your legs and licking swiftly with my tongue over what I was certain was your well-engorged clit. And then, I would have slid you all the way down on your back and climbed over you. My cock was hungry to meet your cunt. So damn hungry I could hardly bear to sit back and watch the show.

Now, your thumb joined the act, rubbing around and around in quick, darting circles over what must have been your clit. I couldn't see it, however, because your thumb shielded it from view.

"You've told people?" I asked softly, not wanting you to stop. You were angelic there, on the floor, your breathing coming faster now. I could see that you were growing closer to your peak because your cheeks had a warm, pink glow and your lips were parted. It was more difficult for you to make yourself meet my eyes when you spoke. You could, in fact, barely keep them focused on me.

"No..." you said, a rush of breath. A third finger joined the first two inside you, and I could just guess that you were squeezing these fingers with your inner muscles. "No... people don't know about it. But you—" now you took a deep breath. "You're a critic. You would have guessed. Right?"

I shook my head, then bent at your side and began to run my fingers over your body, tracing your ribs, the flat smooth line of your belly, using my own fingers to part your pussy lips and look inside at the true work of art, the gradations of color so mysterious, dark, deep pink, a fabulously rich hue.

"Can you imagine?" you whispered, "Can you imagine watching me dipping a paintbrush into my cunt... and then sweeping it across a finished work, creating this mystical, glossy shine?"

I shook my head. But really, as you spoke, I could do just what you said. I could see you doing exactly what you described. You arched your back and shuddered, then, coming, I could tell, because I was helping you. Artists are like all other members of the performance family: actors, singers, comedians—they always need an audience.

"Will you reveal it?" you said next, trying to collect yourself, but obviously still cresting from your climax. "Will you reveal me?"

I shook my head, somewhat dazed from this show, this display. But then, as you dressed yourself, as you returned to the main part of the gallery, I grabbed you by the shoulders and pulled you close. This time, pressing my lips to your ear, I whispered, "I would like to buy one of your paintings..."

Your face lit with a smile.

"But I would like you to do a self-portrait for me."

And now that smile broadened, and you nodded. "A special painting," you whispered back. "One that you can only exhibit privately."

Love Letter

My baby, my darling. My green-eyed girl. You want me, I know it. The way you look at me when you think I don't see you. The way you stare at me, your eyes following the lines of my body, carefully, consistently. Don't worry, chica. I see you.

And I know.

You have a special way of gazing at me when you're in a naughty mood. That hint of a blush on your cheeks as you stare up from under your long dark lashes. I like that look, the guilty quality in it, the way your cheeks flush rosy pink when I catch you staring.

Maybe you think that I can't tell your deepest desires. Maybe nobody ever has before. You've probably given a few hints, tried to make it subtly clear what you like, to no avail. Don't worry about me. You don't have to explain anything. When two people know each other as well as we do, it's easy to decipher the wants and needs, even those that aren't spoken aloud.

You want someone to spank you. I can do that. I can take care of that yearning. You want someone strong and dominant who will put you over his firm knee, slide your little skirt up and your little panties down and spank that naughty ass of yours for you. Don't worry, bella. You're already naked to me. There is nothing ugly about the X-rated fantasies that bring you the most pleasure when you're alone in bed, your fingers working rabbit-quickly against your clit, your breathing harsh and fast. There's nothing inside you that could frighten me.

Nothing at all.

You can confess everything to me. You can close your eyes and kneel at the foot of your bed. You can say, "Bless me, Sir, for I have sinned..." and I will listen to all of your dirty deeds, and I will cleanse you of them. Rest assured that your punishment will suit the crime, that you will receive the pain you need, the humiliation you require.

And then, as tears streak your pretty, most falsely innocent face, I will bestow upon you incredible pleasures. More sweet tenderness than you can imagine, than you could ever possibly deserve. Once you take your punishment, like a good girl, like a *bad* girl, I will make everything better. I will make your cunt throb with pleasure, I will make your thighs wet with the liquid of your sex.

Simply confess to me, darling, and all will be forgiven.

Executive Decision

I was standing in line at the gourmet grocery store, my nearly empty basket containing only a can of plain tomato juice and a bottle of gin. I'd carelessly left my shades in the saddlebag on my motorcycle, which was in the shop this week. So I was squinting, trying to cut the glare from those ever-unfriendly fluorescent lights. I noticed you at first as only a blur, a woman in line behind me emptying your cart onto the rotating wheel, one item after another. I could sense your movements, could sense that you were staring at me, but everything was going slow for me on this day.

Finally, I turned to look your way.

Immediately, I recognized you from the trades, a new executive at one of the studios, and I thought what I'd first thought upon seeing your picture. You're far too pretty to be an executive. Maybe that's sexist, but so be it. My next thought when I saw your picture was that I wanted to fuck you. So now you know. It's how guys think. See a pretty girl; you want to fuck her.

But it was more than that with me. I saw your picture, that glossy black-and-white image, and it stopped me. I liked the way you looked a lot. You were different from starlets and wannabes, the socialites and the celebrity clingers. And you were different from the other few women in your power league. You didn't look as if you were trying to be mannish in order to be in charge. You looked like you knew what you were doing.

Now, that I saw you in person, I had to agree with my initial assumption. First off, I must say that I liked the fact that you were doing your own shopping. And from the items in your cart, it didn't look as if you were picking up forgotten ingredients for some fancy dinner. You were buying actual food.

After summarizing the contents in your cart, I met your eyes. They are a pale green with dark rims, mesmerizing, even in the light of the grocery store. No doubt about it, you were striking, and my type exactly. But I wasn't in the mood. It had been a long night for me, and I was fighting the killerest hangover of my life. All I wanted to do was get home, and climb into bed. Yeah, I wanted to meet you. But I wanted to meet you when I was feeling my best. When I was ready to take whatever you had to dish out. You didn't give me the chance. Instead, you made the first move. Should have expected that, shouldn't I? Someone in your position must be used to going after what you want.

You moved closer to me in line, invading my space. Then you brought your lips to my ear and whispered, "I'm sorry for staring. But you have a look..."

It was a Hollywood line, apropos for budding young starlets hoping to break into the movie biz. You're never supposed to be rude in L.A., on the assumption that you don't know who you're being rude to, could be the next casting director you try out for, the next producer you hope to assist. I must say that I didn't feel well enough to care. I said, "A look? Hmmm... the hungover, slept-in-my-clothes, dumped-by-my-bitch-of-a-girlfriend look?"

I'd thought it would make you back off. Instead, you grinned, your teeth gleamingly bright under those hideous lights, and then you told me to wait for you. To let you buy your groceries—you wanted to talk to me. I liked your attitude. You had balls, if I may use that expression.

"I've got a cab," I said. "My bike died last week."

"Bike? Did you get a flat?"

I sneered. Couldn't help it. You didn't think I pedaled places did you? "Harley," I said, correcting any false assumptions with one simple word.

"I'll drive you where you need to go."

I stumbled into the lot and paid off my driver. Then I waited. Because, fact is, I was even more curious now than I had been on seeing your picture. I don't usually have ladies talk to me the way you did. I look too tough to approach, I think. Most women wait for me to offer an invite for conversation. So once again, I have to say, I liked your style.

You emerged with your small bag of groceries and led me to your Jaguar. Inside, you looked me over again. "There's something..." you muttered to yourself, shrugging, then louder, "You remind me of someone."

So far you'd impressed me at every juncture. Now, I wanted to impress you. Without a word, without any sort of warning at all, I leaned over the seat toward you and kissed you, hard. I cupped your chin with one hand and wrapped my other arm around your slender body, pulling you to me. When you didn't struggle or try to stop me, I moved aside to unbutton your crisp, white blouse, and I began to kiss and nibble at your collar bones, your breasts beneath their underwire lace cups, your flat, toned stomach.

I'll tell you the truth, I would have continued. I would have pushed your limits as far as you would have let me, but after a moment, you said, "Wait," put the car in drive, and shuttled us to an alley several minutes away. Then you lay back again, ready for me to do my duty. Instead, I opened the car door and exited, staring at you through the windshield until you followed me.

We were behind some of the biggest mansions in Beverly Hills. The alley was wider than many city streets and completely deserted except for a lone Persian housecat checking the scene. I pressed your hands against the stucco wall of the nearest chateau wall, breathing in as I did to catch the fragrant wisteria drooping above us. Then I stripped you, leaving each article of your clothing on the hood of your fancy car. You didn't protest. I liked that.

I freed my cock, spit on my fingers, and lubed the length. I needn't have bothered. Your cunt was nice and liquid for me, as fragrant as the pale, purple blossoms that dropped on us from above. I slid my tool between your thighs from behind. I like going at it like that, in that animal way. I rocked it in deep, then grabbed you around the waist and used your body on mine, moving you forward and back, setting the pace with the rhythm of my heartbeat.

You were almost totally silent as we fucked, much different than my recent ex-lover whose faux screams had caused our neighbors to alert 911 on more than one occasion. You were unusually self-contained, but I could sense when you neared your peak. Your body grew still in my hands, your muscles became taut, and your skin seemed to glow beneath the warm, California sunlight.

I liked the way your naked body looked against my black-clad form. I liked how wet you were making my slacks when you pressed back against me.

Most important, I have to say, I liked you not knowing who I was. Unless I revealed myself earlier, you wouldn't know until you saw the trades in the morning. Isn't that how this world always works? See it in print and it becomes real.

When you came, violent shudderings filled you and then subsided, slowly, leaving you breathless. You turned to look at me, head tilted again, and your green eyes were positively shining. I stood there, leaning on your car, watching and waiting to see when you'd place me. But you were off in your own world. Quietly, you got dressed, those stunning eyes focused on me. I opened the door of your car, grabbed my package, and headed down the alley.

"I'll drive you home," you called out to me. "Hey–" and then a silence, when you realized that you didn't even know my name. Had that happened to you before? Had you ever fucked a stranger? You didn't look like the type, but then you'd shocked me already this afternoon—how many other tricks did you have up your sleeve? Now, was my turn to shock you.

I pulled my keys from my pocket and unlocked the back gate to my house. "No problem," I said, grandly, sure that you'd follow after me, that I'd make you a Bloody Mary and we could talk all about work together— "I'm already here."

The Rules of the Game

I see you across the lobby, and you look incredible. You're wearing a little electric-blue dress that I've never seen you wear before—it's so tight and short and low-cut that you look like a high-class call girl. The black bolero jacket doesn't diminish that impression—it's equally tight, accenting the swell of your full breasts in the snug, low-cut dress. You make such a fetching hooker that I almost guess the rules of the game, but you keep me duped for another few moments as I watch you sauntering toward me, a knowing smile on your full, red-painted lips. You've got a little string of pearls on, not to mention a pair of black sheer stockings and highheeled shoes.

I understand—or, rather, I think I understand—why you asked me here, dressed up in an Armani suit and carrying a roll of hundred-dollar bills, to the lobby of the city's best hotel at 10:00 on a Tuesday night. A late dinner in the hotel restaurant, perhaps—which has been getting rave reviews lately from the local papers—and then a booty call in a hotel suite. The idea intrigues me, though I might have been just as happy to meet you in your apartment, where of late I've had the best sex of my life. Thinking about that, I can feel my cock stirring in my pants, already, before you even take the barstool next to me.

"This seat taken?" you ask, once you're situated comfortably.

"No," I say, smiling. I'm about to say "Hi" and hug you, call you by your name. But before I can, you speak.

"I'm Simone," you tell me, putting out your hand for me

to either shake it or kiss it. I'm taken aback at first: That's not your name at all. Not a middle name, nickname or alias—at least, not that I know of. Then it hits me—what you're doing, you naughty little thing.

"Pleased to meet you, ah, *Simone*," I tell you. I take your hand and kiss it. "I'm....Mike."

"Nice to meet *you*, *Mike*." Your lips curve around the word with contempt, telling me that you would know it was an alias even if we *hadn't* been sleeping together for months. "In town for the convention?"

I have to grope for the response, because it's just then that I've realized you're not wearing your usual scent—instead, it's something expensive but tawdry, suggestive and inviting.

"Yeah," I say nervously. "I'm in town for the convention." My head spins as I breathe in your scent, excited by the game you're playing. As you shift on the barstool, I see your short dress riding up slightly, and I notice you've got garters attached to your lace-top stockings. I find myself wondering what else you're wearing under that tiny dress.

"What can I get you?" asks the bartender, a pert college-age girl wearing a white tuxedo shirt.

You look at me, raise your eyebrows.

"Can I buy you a drink?" I blurt nervously.

A charming, gracious smile crosses your face. "I'd love that. I'll have a Cosmopolitan."

Of course you will, I think, and I order another Johnnie Walker Black, neat. You've never ordered a Cosmopolitan since I've known you, but what else would a high-class whore order?

"I love the taste of Scotch," you say. "It's so sexy on a man's lips."

I swallow nervously. This should be easy, smooth—after all, it's no surprise that you've seduced me into another erotic adventure. But I find my breath coming tight in my chest, my heart pounding as if you were really a stranger. Is it the scent? The clothes? Or the lascivious way you're looking at me, telling me that I'm nothing more than prey for you to run down, capture, and devour?

"Do you work around here?" I ask.

"You could say that," you smile.

The bartender brings the drinks, and without missing a beat I pay for them and tip her with a five-dollar bill. She thanks me warmly and gives both of us a disapproving look—but her eyes linger longer on you, the whore of Babylon turning this expensive hotel into a two-bit bordello.

I drink half the Scotch while you sip gingerly at your Cosmo. "That's a very nice suit you're wearing," you tell me. "Your wife must help you shop."

I laugh uncomfortably, and only half of it is an act.

"Girlfriend?"

"Well," I say. "I've got a girlfriend."

"No kidding," you say, your lips toying with the cocktail straw. "I guess that's not a surprise with a guy like you. You know what they say."

"What do they say?" I gulp the rest of the Scotch and the bartender refills it without asking.

"All the good ones are taken. Your girlfriend's obviously a very lucky lady, Mike. Been together long?"

"Almost a year," I say. Then I smile. "She's great, but she could be a little more adventurous."

I see your eyes narrow, and I know that with that simple statement I've changed the rules of the game, hooking you with the promise of forbidden knowledge—however counterfeit—and reeling you in before you even know it.

But you remain cool, playing it to the hilt.

"Adventurous, Mike?"

"You know....in bed."

"Oh," you say, sipping at your drink. "*Sexually* adventurous."

"That's right," I say. "I hope I haven't shocked you."

You giggle, your lips pursing as you stare at me.

"Oh, no, Mike," you sigh. "I doubt anything you could say would shock me."

"Oh, that's a relief," I say.

"I mean, what is it your girlfriend doesn't want to do?" you ask me. "Whatever it is, I'm sure there's a girl out there who would be happy to oblige."

"You think? Just the other night, I wanted to hang from the chandeliers. And she said to me, 'But honey, what about the security deposit?'"

"Really."

I drink my Scotch, smiling at you.

"Well, I'm sure all sexually potent men such as yourself have some things their wives or girlfriends won't do. For instance, it's a well-known fact that most men need a good hard spanking, isn't it?"

"Is it?"

"Yes," you say, pursing your lips. "A really good hard one. Especially when they're being smart-asses, which certain men do with great regularity."

"Is that so?"

You smile and laugh. "Then again, if they're adventurous themselves, they should really be rewarded, don't you think? After all, some women really *like* it when a man wants naughty things. Chandeliers aside."

"Some women?"

"Uh-huh." Your tongue teases the cocktail straw, your eyes undressing me over the rim of the glass.

The bartender is frowning at us. "Another Cosmo, Ma'am?"

"Please," I say. "Allow me."

"Of course. Thank you." You smile at the bartender, and blow her a kiss. She reddens and looks away.

"So what naughty things do you *really* want, Mike? You aren't fooling me with that comment about the chandeliers. I bet there's something really dirty that you're just dying to try, isn't there?"

"Well," I say. "There isn't really anything...."

"Oh, come now. Something you wouldn't dare ask your wife? I mean girlfriend?"

"Girlfriend," I say.

"Something you think she'd never do?"

"Well," I say.

"Come on," you say. "I'm a total stranger. You can admit everything to me, and no one will ever know. And don't tell me it's something like oral sex—I'm sure your girlfriend knows how to provide on that count."

"Oh yes," I say quickly. "She's....she's incredible."

"Really," you smile. "She gives good head?"

I glance around surreptitiously, making sure no one can hear.

"In-fucking-credible," I say. "She gives the best head I've ever had."

You giggle. "You should never tell that to a woman you've just met, Mike. She might take it as a challenge."

"No kidding."

"Come on," you say teasingly. "You're changing the subject. True confessions time."

"You first."

"Oh, now it's about me?" You lean close to me on the barstool. "You want to know what I fantasize about?"

"I'll show you mine if you show me yours."

Our eyes meet, and for an instant it's almost like I *don't* know you, like this complex game we're playing has opened up a new woman inside you.

"Are you faithful, Mike?"

"To my girlfriend?"

"Of course."

"Oh, absolutely," I say.

"Because that's what I fantasize about," you say softly, leaning even closer to make sure no one can hear. "Finding a man such as yourself, a really....good looking, sexy man, successful..."

"Um, thanks," I say, reddening.

"A man who would never, ever think about cheating on his girlfriend; a man who's totally, completely trustworthy. And making him go mad with lust, so mad that he can't control himself, that he betrays his girlfriend without even thinking about it."

I stare into your eyes, my heart pounding.

"Don't you think that would be sexy, *Mike*?"

"I...I don't know."

"Don't you think it would be sexy to totally lose everything, lose all hope of being the man you want to be, and just totally give yourself over to some slut in a hotel room? Some woman you've never met before?"

Now I'm breathing hard, and when I down the last of my Scotch the bartender doesn't refill it. She's over on the far end of the bar, polishing glasses and scowling at us.

"Yes," I say, leaning close and putting my hand in the small of your back. "I guess that would be sexy."

You sigh, pulling away and reaching back to gently push my hand away. "Of course, it's just a fantasy," you say, and tip your empty glass to the bartender. She doesn't look happy at all about getting you another drink, but she sets us both up and I toss a Jackson on the bar. She ignores it.

"Just a fantasy," you say sadly, your tongue toying with the rim of your glass.

"It doesn't have to be," I say.

You look into my eyes again and smile.

"It doesn't?"

"No," I say.

"But you just told me you were faithful. I assumed you were completely out of my league. I mean, you would never want to—"

"Please," I say. "Let's get a room."

You laugh. "Now, Mike....you're not going to tell me you're thinking of cheating on your girlfriend, are you? You just told me she gives you the best head you've ever had."

"She does," I say. "Incredible."

"You're going to risk all that for a few hours in a hotel room with a woman you don't even know? You must think I'll give you even better head."

My cock is so hard, now, I'm afraid I won't be able to walk to the front desk. "Please," I say. "I'll get a room. On me."

"Well, Mike....I'm afraid I've got to leave for the airport in just a few minutes. I couldn't possibly miss my flight."

"Please," I tell you. "Please stay. I'd love to get to know you better."

"I bet you would," you say, now leaning away from me and turning your shoulders so you're facing the bartender rather than me. She's begun to ignore us completely.

"Can't you change your flight?"

"I'm afraid it's non-refundable."

You're so good, I could almost believe you really are a callgirl. You've reeled me in, and a strong force within me believes that you're really ready to walk out the door leaving me panting with desire, unsatisfied and angry. It's so complicated, so intricate, I want to laugh. But I don't, because this game has gotten serious, and the throbbing of my cock in my pants is telling me that there's no chance, now, that either one of us is willing to lose.

"I'll pay for your flight," I say.

You turn back toward me, arching your back so your breasts stretch invitingly through the fabric of your little blue dress. I can see your nipples, erect, and rather than telling me that you're as turned on as I am, that you're as vulnerable as me, what I see in them is my own inexorable lust, leading me into a manufactured Gehenna of sin and damnation. And I don't care. I just want you, want to wrap my lips around each of those firm nipples and taste them. Want to slide that little blue dress off of you and bear your body, naked, deep into the softness of these expensive hotel beds.

"Oh, I couldn't let you do that."

"I'll pay for your flight...and your hotel room."

"Now, Mike, surely you know that I'm not going to share a room with you—I barely know you."

"I'll get you another room." You're my girlfriend, but I'm so consumed by desire for you I wouldn't dream of reminding myself that I can have you any night at home. I want you here, now, upstairs in a rented room.

"Well," you say, leaning toward me again, your hand resting in my lap, your fingertips brushing my cock. "We'll see about that. For now, maybe you should just get one."

"How much?"

"How much what, Mike?"

"How much is your flight?"

"Five hundred dollars," you say.

"Even?"

"Yes," you tell me. "Five hundred dollars even. Do you have the cash?"

"Yes," I say.

"You expected me."

"I'll get a room."

You lean closer, your breath sweet in my face. "All right. Bring me back one of the keys and leave the cash by the door when you go in the room. I'll meet you in a few minutes."

"Don't go anywhere," I tell you.

"Oh, Mike," you say softly, your lips just barely brushing mine. "I wouldn't dream of it."

I know it's all a game; I made love to you just last night, to our overwhelming mutual satisfaction. But I feel like I've stumbled into your darkest fantasy, the edge you walk when you're feeling bad. And you're good at it—better than I could have dreamed. The strange thing is, I don't care. I don't care that it's artifice, that we're lovers and you're as far from being a call girl as a woman can be. I don't care at all—I just care that I have to have you, right now, in a hotel room, calling you "Simone" and paying you $500 to fuck me.

When I return to the bar, you're sitting there chatting with the bartender, who seems to have become more friendly since I left. The two of you are laughing together like old friends.

I come over to your barstool, take your hand, press the key into it. I lean forward to kiss you, but you turn your face and receive my kiss on your cheek.

Your act is impressive—no money's changed hands, so I don't get a thing. I smile at you, my cock hard in my pants.

"See you upstairs?" I whisper.

"Yes, darling," you say. "I'll just be a few minutes." You wink at the bartender, who blushes.

When I open the door, I'm greeted by that familiar smell of a clean hotel room. I shut the door behind me and turn on the light next to the king-sized bed. I angle it toward the wall—mood lighting.

I'm not sure what to do next—do I greet you with a drink in my hand? Do I take you in my arms as you walk in the door? Either of those would seem hopelessly out of place, so I go with the most direct route I can think of.

I take off my clothes.

Fishing out the five hundred-dollar bills you told me to bring, I fan them out on the dresser near the door. The smell of the money makes me even harder. My cock feels pained, desperate for your touch. Looking at the five bills, I walk back to the rumpled mess of my suit pants and fish out my wallet. I take out as many twenties as I can find, put ten of them crosswise atop the fanned hundreds. Consider it a tip— in good faith, because I know this is going to be the fuck of my life.

I decide to take a shower; I rinse off quickly, not bothering with soap, then towel dry as I drip my way to the bed. I toss the towel in the corner and peel back the covers. The sheets feel cold against my naked body, rough and starched against my cock. Every inch of my flesh feels alive with sensation and anticipation. My heart pounds as I await the arrival of my well-paid whore.

When I hear the key in the door, I can't help but squirm against the sheets. I think in that moment I want you more than I've ever wanted any woman in my life. My cock pulses with the sound of your key scraping in the lock.

You enter the dimly-lit hotel room. When you pick up the money, you sigh.

"You're very generous, Mike," you tell me, tucking the bills into your purse. "Generous as well as handsome."

"Thank you."

"What do you want to do, Mike?"

"Make love to you."

You laugh, bringing your hand to your mouth as if you can't believe I've just said it. "Oh, Mike. I doubt that."

"All right," I say. "I want to fuck you."

"Really. Is that all?"

"I want to fuck you so hard you scream," I say. "I want to fuck your pussy until you come so many times you cry."

You smile. "Does your girlfriend let you talk like that?"

"She encourages it."

"She must be a naughty girl. Naughty and very horny."

"Exceptionally so, Simone."

You walk to the side of the bed, setting your purse on the dresser and shrugging off your little jacket. The dress clings to your breasts and I can see your nipples, erect with excitement. You come over to the side of the bed and bend down slightly, turning away from me.

"Unzip me, will you?" you ask, your voice soft and seductive.

I draw your zipper down to the small of your back, exposing the strap of your lacy bra. You walk around to the foot of the bed and peel the dress away, slowly revealing your body. God, it's incredible. I always want you when I see you take your clothes off, but now it's particularly acute—I'm practically insane with desire. Your black bra is cut so low and tight that your breasts are spilling out, your nipples having already made their way through the flimsy spray of lace on the edges of the half-cups. Your matching thong is skimpy and descends to the point where I could see your pubic hair if you hadn't trimmed so assiduously. The black garter belt frames your crotch deliciously, and I notice that you've put the thong on over your garters.

You crawl onto the bed, straddling me as you make your way up to me and pull down the sheets. Bending down, you brush your breasts against my chest, kissing my neck.

"I want you to fuck me," you whisper. "Any way you want. I'm yours for the night."

I wrap my arms around you and pull you tight to me. Our lips meet and I taste the vodka, lime and triple sec on your tongue. My hands cradle your bare ass and you push it back into my grasp, arching your back as you draw your breasts up to my face. I suckle your hard nipples gently as you reach under the sheets and take hold of my cock, wrapping your slender fingers around my shaft and squeezing. Hungrily, you begin to stroke me. Before I know it, you've buried yourself under the tangled sheets and I feel your mouth on my cock, hot and slippery. You take me into your mouth and your lips descend until they're almost wrapped around the base of my shaft. I reach out to grab your waist and guide you around. I pull down your thong and you wriggle out of it; I see that you're not only trimmed, you're shaved. You reverse your position on top of me and spread your legs around my face, gently settling your pussy onto my mouth. I taste your sharp, musky cunt and my tongue finds your clit, teasing it as I hear your moan muffled around the shaft of my cock. Your hips grind back and forth as my lips mold to yours, your juices flowing as your smooth pussy rides my face.

You take your time, because you're an expert. Certainly you know the exact way to make me come, but in this persona you know the way to make *any* man come, and it's clear you don't want me to come yet. Your mouth moves in just the right rhythm to build me close, bringing me to the edge of orgasm as your head bobs up and down on me. Then, without warning, you slow, slip my cock out of your mouth and tease the head with the very tip of your tongue, letting me cool down so you can savor my hard cock for as long as you want. I, however, am not nearly so charitable. I want you to come, and come now, because I'm hungry to feel your body bucking on top of me, your hips pumping your cunt against my face as you desperately suck my cock. I focus on your clit, only licking down to your tight opening so I can taste the flowing juices of your pussy. You're wet, incredibly wet—I noticed that from the first moment your pussy touched my lips. And I can tell from the way you're moving that you're close; you're going to come.

Of course, I know it doesn't matter—a good whore will always fake an orgasm when her client is eating her, right? Never having had such an experience, I savor the knowledge that even if you weren't going to come, you'd pretend—after all, I've paid for you to enjoy yourself even more than I've paid for me to enjoy myself, because my ego demands it; my ego demands that you come, moaning, on my face.

Except that I know you could never fake it as good as you'd have to fake it to convince me, for real. I know you could never fake the way your whole body twists and writhes on top of me, the way your mouth, anxiously seeking my cock, dissolves into a pair of lips thoughtlessly, hopelessly working without the barest hint of control. You could never fake the way your thighs tighten around my face, the way your back arches, the way your breath comes tight in your throat and you shiver on top of me.

You could never fool me with the way you come.

Or could you?

I don't care. For now, it's real, and I want it. I want it so bad I suckle your clit steadily through the whole mounting rise of your climax, my tongue seething against it as you whimper "I'm going to come....I'm going to come...don't stop!" and then your body goes taut, jerking wildly, and you push your cunt down onto my face, so hard it hurts me, so hard it almost suffocates me as you pump your hips madly. When you slump forward onto me, my cock, slippery with your spit, presses between your breasts, rubbing on the satin lace of your bra. You're panting desperately. You sound like you're about to cry.

"Oh God....oh God," you moan. "Mike, you're so good...oh god, you eat pussy so good...where'd you learn to eat pussy like that?"

I place my hands on your hips, lift your body slightly so I can slide out from under you. My cock, hard and slick, glistening in the light from the nightstand, is ready for you.

"From my girlfriend," I say as I position myself behind you. "She's very demanding."

I don't tease you at all; I enter you in one thrust, because I can't stand to be outside of you for one more instant. Your pussy is so wet I can feel the juice dribbling out of it, so tight from your muscles clenching in orgasm that I almost have to force my cock in. But you gasp as I enter you, and you lift your ass in the air, pushing back onto me, shoving your tight pussy over my cock until I can feel the head grinding against your familiar cervix, until I can feel your lips stretched tight around the base of my shaft. God, it feels incredible. Your pussy is so hot around my cock I feel I'm about to be burned, but that doesn't stop me from drawing back almost all the way and then fucking you, hard, a single thrust that sends a spasm through your gorgeous body, and lifts your ass high as you leave your face pressed against the bed and reach back with your hands to spread your lips wide for me, inviting me deeper.

I thrust into you again, hard, and your legs spread further, your feet kicking involuntarily and sending the pillows flying to opposite sides of the room. The next thrust brings your ass up still higher, elicits a shuddering moan from your lips. You're still spreading your lips wide, begging me to enter you deeper, to fuck you harder. You whisper "Yes…yes…yes…yes…god, Mike, your cock's so big, it's so fucking big I almost can't take it, Mike…god, it feels so good, so huge…your girlfriend's such a lucky girl, Mike, to have a guy with such a big cock…oh god, it's so huge…so fucking huge in my tight, wet pussy…"

Normally you would never moan like that in the middle of lovemaking; a woman entirely engrossed in the sexual sensations of the body, you limit your dirty talk to articulate moans and whimpers of pleasure, telling me all I need to know. But you've adapted the methods of your new persona, and while "Simone" is lifting her ass high to encourage me deeper into her pussy, she's also telling me how well-hung I am. Strangely, the sound of your voice uttering such obscenities excites me more, and I start fucking you harder, faster, encouraged to new heights of need by each word you utter. I know I'm going to come soon, but I want my whore to come, too, to come on my cock as I thrust into her, feeling her pussy clench tight around my shaft. I reach under you and find your clit with my fingertips, its familiar contour inviting a familiar stroke. But Simone is a different woman, and you whisper "Oh God…rub me harder, harder, Mike, rub my clit harder, fuck me harder, fuck my wet pussy harder with your big fat cock!" I don't think I've ever heard you say the words "wet pussy" or "big fat cock" in all the time we've been together, and the filthiness, the silliness of it, draws me further in to the illusion; I start rubbing your clit so hard I'm afraid I might hurt you, fucking you so hard I *know* I'm going to hurt you if I keep going—but you just beg me for more, encouraging me deeper into my passion as you pump back against me, your hands long since having left your pussy lips, no longer holding them open, knowing I need no encouragement to slide my cock deep into you. Now, your hands are flat against the bed, helping to push you back onto my cock, to meet every thrust I give you with one of your own, equally hard, equally demanding. Coaxed by the pressure on your clit and the familiar curve of my cock against your G-spot, I know you're going to come. And this time, as before, I'm quite sure you're not faking.

You tell me every sensation as it goes through your body. "I'm coming, Mike….fuck…I'm coming on your huge cock, coming—you're hitting my G-spot, Mike, you're hitting me deep—fuck me harder, fuck me harder!" And then those dirty words disintegrate into incoherent moans of ecstasy, as I feel the muscles of your pussy contracting in rapid motions around my cock, milking me, begging me for my come even as you climax yourself, moaning on my cock.

I can't hold back any longer. My fingers still working your clit in time with the thrusts of our sweat-slick bodies, I match the rhythm of my hips to my own needs, the exact speed that will make me come—and within a few more thrusts, I'm doing it, coming deep inside you, hearing you beg for it—"Come inside me, Mike, come inside me, oh yes, give me your come!"—as I let go. When I go rigid and then relax on top of you, I feel my body sliding effortlessly against yours, both of us sheened with sweat. I kiss the back of your neck.

"Your girlfriend's very lucky," you sigh. "What's her name?"

"Simone," I tell you.

You laugh.

"What a strange coincidence. The same name as me."

"Isn't it, though?"

I get a wake-up call at seven the next morning—the exact time I would normally get up for work.

You're gone, a faint depression in the bed where your naked body stretched out next to mine, exhausted after we'd made love for the third time—a mere three hours ago. There's a note, written on hotel stationery in handwriting I don't recognize. Neat trick, that.

If you ever need company when you're in town, give me a call, Mike. I had a great time. Your girlfriend's a very lucky lady. Hope it lasts.
Love,
Simone
XXXOOOXXX

Underneath is written a phone number with a pager code. It's none of the numbers you use, not your work pager, home phone or cell phone.

Under the note is your skimpy black lace thong, still moist with the juice of your pussy.

I resist the urge to call you all day, but I'm a little surprised that you don't call me. When I get back to my apartment from work that evening, though, I recognize a telltale scent in the air—your scent, not Simone's. The scent I recognize as your signature, the one I savor as it lingers in my apartment for hours after you've left.

The door to my bedroom is closed.

There on the coffee table are five hundreds, fanned out. Across them is a stack of twenties, and when I count them, I find there's $400, an extra ten $20 bills from what I tipped you.

I smile to myself and look at the closed bedroom door. Tucking the bills into my pocket, I unknot my tie.

Clearly you've changed the rules of the game, and upped the ante.

But then, the stakes were always higher than a simple $700.

I strip off my clothes and walk, nude, into the bedroom.

About the Authors

Thomas Roche is a worker-owner at San Francisco's Good Vibrations and the author of more than 150 published short stories that have appeared in such publications as the *Best American Erotica* series, the *Mammoth Book of Erotica* series, and many other anthologies, magazines and websites. His web projects have included work on Good Vibes Magazine (www.goodvibes.com), Universal Studios' 13th Street (13thstreet.com), and Gothic Net (www.gothic.net). Books he has edited include three volumes of the *Noirotica* series of erotic crime-noir and the soon-to-be-released *Best Men's Erotica* (Cleis). His own short story collections include *Dark Matter* and two collaborations with Alison Tyler, *His* and *Hers*.

Alison Tyler is a shy girl with a dirty mind. She is the author of more than 15 sexy novels including *Learning to Love It*, *Strictly Confidential*, *Sweet Thing*, and *Sticky Fingers* (all published by Black Lace) and *The ESP Affair* and *Blue Valentine* (published by Magic Carpet Books). Her short stories have appeared in anthologies including *Sweet Life*, *Erotic Travel Tales I & II*, *Best Women's Erotica 2002 & 2003*, *Best Fetish Erotica*, and *Best Lesbian Erotica 1996* (all published by Cleis), as well as *Wicked Words 4, 5 & 6* (Black Lace). She was a runner-up in *Penthouse Variations* Baudelaire Fiction Contest. Ms. Tyler lives with her partner of seven years in the San Francisco Bay Area—but she misses L.A.